Freya and the Magic Jewel

**ALSO BY
JOAN HOLUB & SUZANNE WILLIAMS**

The Goddess Girls series

The Heroes in Training series

Thunder Girls

BOOK 1

Freya and the Magic Jewel

JOAN HOLUB &
SUZANNE WILLIAMS

Aladdin

New York   London   Toronto   Sydney   New Delhi

ALADDIN

An imprint of Simon & Schuster Children's Publishing Division
1230 Avenue of the Americas, New York, New York 10020
First Aladdin hardcover edition May 2018
Text copyright © 2018 by Joan Holub and Suzanne Williams
Jacket illustration copyright © 2018 by Pernille Ørum
Interior illustration of tree copyright © 2018 by Elan Harris

For information about special discounts for bulk purchases, please contact
Simon & Schuster Special Sales at 1-866-506-1949 or business@simonandschuster.com.
The Simon & Schuster Speakers Bureau can bring authors to your live event. For more information or to book an event contact the Simon & Schuster Speakers Bureau at 1-866-248-3049 or visit our website at www.simonspeakers.com.
Designed by Laura Lyn DiSiena
The text of this book was set in Baskerville.
Manufactured in the United States of America 0318 FFG
2 4 6 8 10 9 7 5 3 1
Library of Congress Cataloging-in-Publication Data
Names: Holub, Joan, author. | Williams, Suzanne, 1953- author.
Title: Freya and the magic jewel / by Joan Holub and Suzanne Williams.
Description: First Aladdin hardcover edition. | New York : Aladdin, 2018. |
Series: Thunder Girls ; book 1 | Summary: Unlike her twin brother Frey, twelve-year-old girlgoddess Freya is not excited about their invitation to Asgard Academy, especially after she loses her magical jewel, leaving her powerless and worried about making friends.
Identifiers: LCCN 2017053753 |
ISBN 9781481496407 (hc) | ISBN 9781481496414 (eBook)
Subjects: | CYAC: Mythology, Norse—Fiction. | Friendship—Fiction. | Magic—Fiction. | Lost and found possessions—Fiction. | Schools—Fiction. |
BISAC: JUVENILE FICTION / Legends, Myths, Fables / Norse. | JUVENILE FICTION / Girls & Women. | JUVENILE FICTION / Social Issues / Friendship.
Classification: LCC PZ7.H7427 Fre 2018 | DDC [Fic]—dc23
LC record available at https://lccn.loc.gov/2017053753

Til Heidi,
mitt kjære barnebarn i Norge
—S. W.

For Thunder Girls everywhere
who make some noise
—J. H.

For our amazing readers.
Thunder on!

McKenna W., Andrade Family, Amelia G., Shelby J.,
Virginia J., Samantha J., Kalista B., Claire B., Charlotte S.,
Emma J., McKay O., Reese O., Emeleia M., Jenny C., Lillia L.,
Rachel L., Mackenzie S., Evilynn R., Olivia R., Caysin U.,
Ariel P., Megan D., Aurora-Joyce P., Elia P., Holly N.,
Tatiana T., Keny Y., Kasidy Y., Koko Y., Lily-Ann (Red) S.,
Kira L., Maddie A., Samantha K., Kaysyn J., Brienna J.,
Olivia M., Haley G., Riley G., Renee G., Stephanie T.,
Meghan B., Medori W., Maddie A., M., Brynn S., Lori F.,
Ellis T., Ava Lee S., Caitlin R., Hannah R., Sofia W.,
Olive Jean D., Fe Susan D., Sarah D., Patricia D., Khanya S.,
Olivia C., Malia C., Emily and Grondine Family,
the Saleeby girls—Sassy, Elle, and Josi—Violet L., Kristen S.,
and you.

—J. H. and S. W.

Contents

1
Jewel

Meow! meow!

"Fly, kitty, kitty!" the girlgoddess Freya called to her magical gray tabby cats. Her long pale-blond hair fanned out behind her as she urged them onward. The red cart they pulled soared a half-dozen feet above the snowy ground, around tree trunks and under branches, sometimes barely missing big, mossy boulders. It wasn't easy to get this pair of pony-size cats to fly the cart in the direction she wanted them to go!

Upon reaching a familiar forest path lined with ferns, she called out, "Whoa, kitty, kitty!" To her relief, the cats obeyed and set down in the snow. "Good job, *silfrkatter*," she said, using the Norse word that meant "silver cats." "Our first trip together. And we made it!" She leaned forward to pat the cats' soft fur, and they purred happily.

Remembering why she'd come all this way, Freya jumped from the cart and commanded, "Catnap!"

Plink! If anyone had been watching at that moment, the cats and cart would've seemed to instantly disappear. However, in reality, they had only shrunk down to a single cat's-eye marble. Freya's twin brother, the boygod Frey, had given her the colorful marble as a gift only yesterday, on her twelfth birthday.

She snatched the marble from the air before it could fall to the snowy ground. Then she slipped it into one of several fist-size pouches that dangled from the nine necklaces of beads, seeds, or metal chain that she wore. Each necklace held one or more items, such as keys, small tools, or special keepsakes.

Nine was a lucky, super-special number. Because as everyone knew, there were nine worlds altogether in the Norse universe. All were located on three enormous, ring-shaped levels stacked one above the other. Vanaheim, the world where Freya lived, was only *one* of those worlds!

Freya's breath made quick fog-puffs in the cold air as she crossed the path and stepped into a small hut. It was the home of the old sorceress Gullveig, who she and her brother called *amma*. That meant "grandmother," though Gullveig was really their nanny, not a relative. Once inside, Freya saw that the hut was still as empty as it had been for the last five months. Her shoulders slumped in disappointment.

She pulled a walnut-size jewel shaped like a teardrop from another necklace pouch and stared at it. It was pale orange now, which meant it felt unsettled, like she did. While in her possession, it changed colors according to her mood!

"Tell me, jewel Brising, where is Gullveig?" she asked it. "Did she find the gold she was looking for in Asgard?"

Her jewel's voice came as a low, magical humming sound that only she could hear and understand:

> *"Gold and Gullveig I cannot see.*
> *But here is the vision that comes to me:*
> *Adventure for you is about to start.*
> *In Asgard you must find the heart.*
> *A secret world there hides away*
> *That holds the power to stop doomsday!"*

Startled, Freya stared at the teardrop jewel. "Secret world? Doomsday? I'm not going to Asgard. I'm not! What are you talking about, Brising?" She brought the jewel so close to her nose that her blue eyes almost crossed, wanting it to take back what it had said. It didn't. Although it had the power to show Freya the future, sometimes it only revealed bits of information. It didn't always answer her questions, either, so she could never be sure what it did or didn't know. This time, though, she was positive it was wrong, wrong, wrong. Why would she ever leave Vanaheim? She loved it here!

As Freya stepped out of the hut into the cold air, Brising spoke up again, though she had asked it nothing more. This time it said:

> *"Five months ago a war began.*
> *Five days ago that fight did end.*
> *Five hours ago your fate was sealed—*
> *Five minutes from now 'twill be revealed.*
> *Oops, make that five seconds from now.*
> *One. Two. Three. Four. . . ."*

2
Little Acorn, Big News

***T*HONK!**

"Ow! What in the nine worlds?" Freya jumped in surprise when an acorn beaned her on top of the head outside Gullveig's hut. Silver glitter shimmered in her hair as she rubbed the spot while staring at the acorn, now lying near her feet. All the Vanir (which was what the goddesses and gods of Vanaheim were called) had flecks of silver in their hair that glittered when caught by light.

Quickly Freya poked her jewel back into its white drawstring pouch, which hung from a delicate gold chain. The pouch was a little too heavy for the thin necklace. But it was her very best chain and the only gold one she had. She often got compliments on it. One of these days she should probably hang Brising's pouch on a sturdier, thicker length of gold. However, that wouldn't be easy to find here in Vanaheim. Gold was not at all plentiful in her world, unlike in Asgard (or so she'd heard).

Freya glared at the squirrel that had lobbed the acorn bomb and was scurrying off. "Thanks a lot, Ratatosk!" she called after him. (That was his name, and in her opinion he *was* kind of a rat.) "A friendly 'I'm sorry' might be nice sometime!"

"Say bye-bye!" singsonged the acorn that had beaned her, pulling her attention. It was making tracks down in the snow now, rolling around and around the leather snow boots she wore.

She kneeled and held out a hand, smiling. Message acorns were so adorable, with their cute faces and hats, and sweet voices. This acorn hopped right up onto her palm.

"What should I say bye to?" she asked it.

"To Vanaheim, silly! You are moving. Away! To Asgard!" It gave a happy twirl.

Twin bolts of surprise and dread shot through Freya. Brising had mentioned a trip to Asgard too, but she'd brushed off the idea as goofy. It *was* goofy, right? It had to be.

Asgard was where the most powerful Norse goddesses and gods of all lived. But because of the recently ended war, they were the enemies of Vanaheim. Who wanted to move in with their enemies? Not her!

"No way! I have friends here. I can't just leave!" exclaimed Freya, hoping that what Brising and the acorn had said wasn't really true. Or even if it was, that she still had the choice to remain here in Vanaheim, where everyone and everything were familiar.

The acorn bounced in her hand a few times, saying, "Friends are forever, the most important thing!"

"Yeah, exactly," Freya told it. The acorn wasn't really agreeing with her, she supposed. It must be repeating something it had heard. Message acorns delivered news and were fun, if a little nutty. But their communication skills and intelligence were limited, and this one didn't speak further. Instead it boinged from her hand to the ground and rolled away.

She stood again and watched it head for the nearest oak tree. There were many kinds of trees in the nine worlds besides the oaks that bore acorns. All stood taller than Freya, but they were like tiny twigs compared with the greatest tree of all—Yggdrasil! That ash tree was awesome! And magical! It was nicknamed the World Tree because it was so enormous that it sheltered and protected all nine worlds like a gigantic, leafy umbrella. It had three humongous roots, and a trunk so big around that she figured it would take her entire life to walk all the way around it!

Freya gazed up at that very tree now, missing Gullveig again and feeling let down that she'd been unable to locate her. She tugged her jewel out of its pouch once more and stared at it, unsure how to coax it to reveal Gullveig's whereabouts.

"Brising, I have lots of friends, young and old, and I care about all of them. But Gullveig is like a second mom to Frey and me." Their real mom, Nerthus, was a earth goddess who called no world home. Since water was super important to Yggdrasil, she constantly traveled around the three rings making sure that the World Tree got enough of it. "I mean, Gullveig practically raised Frey and me, you know," Freya went on. "We miss her. We need her, and I'm worried . . ."

Her voice trailed off as a dart of guilt struck her. Because she was pretty sure it was her fault that Gullveig had disappeared! If only Freya hadn't gone

10

on and on about how great gold was when her jewelry club met here five months ago. About how it could be made into such amazing fashion accessories. As the girlgoddess of love and *beauty*, she was into fashion. Still, if only she hadn't wished aloud that she had some Asgard gold so that the club could make more than just silver or wooden jewelry. And most of all, if only Gullveig hadn't overheard her wishing.

Next thing you know, her *amma* had left a note saying she'd gone to Asgard, gold-hunting. Somehow, her quest for gold had set off the war between Vanaheim and Asgard, the only two worlds populated by goddesses and gods. So in a way, all the fighting was Freya's fault, even though everyone blamed Gullveig. But Freya had had no idea how to fix the situation.

Hearing a *scritch, scritch* sound overhead, she glanced up. Ratatosk! He'd returned and was perched on a fir tree branch ten feet overhead, peering down at her and Brising.

"Nosy!" she scolded him.

He only rubbed his front paws together and leaned forward eagerly. "Well, go on. What else were you going to say to that jewel?"

"I was going to ask it why your acorn messages are so squirrelly," she teased, not about to reveal anything more.

Ratatosk straightened, looking miffed. "My acorn spoke the truth to you. A truth I heard straight from the beak of the eagle. So there!"

With that, the squirrel with his knapsack of acorn messengers scampered out of sight back the way he'd come, leaving paw prints in the snow. *Probably off to deliver even nuttier news to someone else,* Freya thought.

He was always running up and down between the worlds, spreading gossip. The eagle-eyed eagle he'd mentioned gathered gossipy news from its perch among the highest branches of Yggdrasil. And Ratatosk was good at getting it to spill that news. But by the time Ratatosk reached Niflheim—the darkest, lowest world of them all—and repeated the news to Nidhogg, the dragon that lived there, the squirrel had usually added juicy tidbits of his own and scrambled things. The gossip he repeated usually made the dragon think the eagle was insulting him. So the dragon would send back fake news that would anger the eagle. It was the squirrel's fault that those two stayed mad at each other!

Once Ratatosk was gone, Freya cupped Brising between her palms. For the bazillionth time she asked, "Where is Gullveig?"

The jewel warmed in her hands. At last! This meant she would see a vision, not just hear a prophecy. Standing in the snow, she glanced around, waiting for a vision to appear that would answer her question.

And one did. But it did not reveal Gullveig's whereabouts. Instead what appeared was a piece of polished wood hovering in the air about two feet from her nose.

As big as her school runebook, it was carved in the shape of a heart with fancy curlicues decorating its edges.

She cocked her head, confused. "Your future-tellings are puzzling today, Brising. A little dis*heart*ening when I'm whole*heart*edly worried over Gullveig." A nervous giggle escaped her.

Giggles gave way to surprise when a single eyeball suddenly materialized within the center of the heart vision! As she studied the eyeball, it studied her back. *Was this Odin's eye?* she wondered in awe. The leader of the Asgard gods and the supreme ruler of all the worlds, he was famous for having only one. And also for being the number one enemy of Vanaheim, despite the war's end.

A voice rumbled out of the heart. "The World Tree needs you, and you need a change. Come to Asgard, and bring your special magic."

Freya gasped. Staring wide-eyed at the eyeball, she

backed up against the door of the hut. "Yggdrasil needs *me*? And my magic?" she squeaked.

"Yes," the voice replied solemnly.

Freya shook her head. Her jewel had magic powers, but she didn't. She'd found it by accident in a clump of clover while looking for the four-leaf kind when she was little. It had been clear like a diamond at first, but the moment she touched it, it had sparked with beautiful colors! Though she'd figured out how to make it speak prophecies, anybody could probably have done the same if they'd found it first. So while it was true that she had power—through Brising—to foresee certain things, that was no big deal.

"Everyone in Vanaheim has some kind of magic talent," she told the vision. "Maybe ask one of the elders instead? Because I'm pretty sure I can't help you, or Yggdrasil, which doesn't even need help, as far as I know. And I don't need a change, either."

The eye blinked at her. It was brown.

Hmm. Wasn't Odin's eye supposed to be blue? Then whose eyeball was this? A stranger's, that's who! It could even be the eye of one of those awful legendary fire giants, for all she knew. Rumor was that they were safely contained in the world of Muspelheim for now. No one around here had ever seen one of them before, so she couldn't be sure that they even existed. But still.

Stuffing her jewel into its pouch, she eased off the hut's porch. She eyed the heart warily, since the vision hadn't yet gone away. "Um, uh . . . thanks for the invitation, but I'm really kind of busy." Then she turned and ran as fast as she could down the path and away from Gullveig's hut.

Poof! She glanced back just in time to see the heart disappear in a puff of white snow powder. What a relief!

When she looked ahead again, a huge, hollow corkscrew vine of translucent green had appeared on the path a few feet before her. A boy with glittery pale-blond hair the exact same color as hers—her twin brother, Frey—was inside it. He was hurtling toward her, coming in for a landing. They were on a crash course!

"Watch out!" Freya yelled, trying to put on the brakes. Too late! Frey spilled out of the bottom end of the vine slide directly in front of her, and she tripped over him. They both tumbled to the snowy ground.

"Ow!" her brother complained as he sprawled on his back. *Schmoop!* His big vine slide shrank to a sprig and dropped onto the path beside him.

"Sorry!" Freya exclaimed, brushing her hair from her eyes.

"S'okay. Are you alone?" Frey looked around quickly as he sat up, like he was expecting someone else to pop out of nowhere.

"Mm-hmm." It didn't surprise her that he was bewildered to find her alone. She usually hung out with tons of friends. The more the merrier! However, today the kids in their village had been busy getting ready for school, since the new semester at Vanaheim Junior High would start tomorrow. She would've been doing the same, if not for her worry over Gullveig.

Frey picked up the sprig of vine and shoved it into his tunic pocket. This vine slide had been *her* birthday gift to *him* yesterday. Brising had helped her find it in a vinefield. No easy task, since it was only a finger-length curlicue of vine most of the time, like now. One that could enlarge back into the huge spiral slide for Frey anytime he wished to travel through it. And then shrink anytime he wasn't using it. She was pleased to see him trying it out, though they obviously both needed more time to master the ins and outs of their birthday gifts. She hoped she would never bump into anyone, like she and Frey had just done, while driving her cart!

Freya stood and brushed snow from her dark-blue linen dress. "Guess what! I just saw an eye in a heart!"

she breathlessly told her brother as he rose to his feet.

"Guess what! We're moving tomorrow!" he said at the same time.

Staring at each other, they both then blurted out, "Wait! What?"

3
An Invitation

"Y**OU GO FIRST,**" F**REY TOLD** F**REYA.**

"I was at Gullveig's hut and thought I saw . . . never mind," she replied, anxious to hear *his* news. "What do you mean, we're *moving*?" Yes, the message acorn had told her that too, but she still didn't want to believe it. But maybe Frey meant to someplace else within Vanaheim? Before she could ask, he went on.

"I came to tell you that the Great and Wonderful Odin sent his two ravens to our village with an invitation," he informed her in a rush. "He wants kids from all nine worlds to go to some new school he's opening. It's called Asgard Academy. Only four kids are invited from Vanaheim. *Including us!*" Frey was practically dancing with excitement.

However, Freya didn't exactly feel like dancing. Not even close.

"You and me? Go to school in Asgard?" she asked, shaking her head. If it was an invitation, they didn't have to go, right? No matter what Brising and the acorn message had predicted.

"Or maybe somewhere near Asgard. Hard to understand raven caws sometimes. Guess we'll find out when we get there." Her brother, who was the boygod of growing things, bent to tend to some star-shaped white wildflowers they'd crushed when they bumped into each other. *Pring!* The stems and petals magically straightened, standing strong and healthy again under his charmed touch.

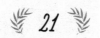

A sinking feeling filled Freya. For once it seemed that Ratatosk and his acorn might have gotten their gossip correct. But the worst news was that Frey *wanted to go*!

She shook her head, sending her pale-blond hair swaying with sparkly glitter. "We can't go. I'm going to be class president, remember? And the Vana Bananas ice-skating team captain! And there's my jewelry club too," she protested.

"Teams and clubs?" Frey huffed, throwing his arms wide. "Is that all you can think about? Going to Asgard will be the coolest thing that's ever happened to us! We'll be fine. Like seeds, we'll bloom where we're planted. Knowing you, you'll make a hundred friends and be in ten clubs by the end of our first week there, probably."

"But . . . ," she sputtered. "I'm not a seed, and I don't want to move away. It's not fair!"

School was starting tomorrow and she had so many plans. Super-popular at Vanaheim Junior High, she had been voted student body president at the end of last

22

year. Not only that, but she had also recently designed the cutest yellow skating outfits for the Vana Bananas and added small yellow pom-poms to the team's white skates. She couldn't wait to hit the ice this year! But how could she carry out those plans if she wasn't here?

"Hello?" Frey said, pulling her attention from her worried daydreaming. Having finished helping the plants, he stood up and dusted the dirt and snow off his hands. "We *have* to go. Odin is the boss," he insisted in a stubborn tone.

"Can't we say no? I thought it was an invitation, not a command," Freya replied just as stubbornly. "The Aesir are our enemies!" (Aesir was what the goddesses and gods of Asgard were called.)

"*Were* our enemies. There's a truce now, remember?"

"But . . ." Hearing soft footsteps behind her, Freya turned to see a family of three reindeer crossing the path close by.

When she turned back, Frey was frowning. He lifted

a blue anemone flower that was hanging its petals like it was super tired. "See this?" he said. "Arguing isn't good for plants. It hurts the dirt, which makes them droopy."

"Huh? Hurts the dirt?" Freya repeated. She giggled. Frey was always saying weird stuff like that. Sometimes by accident and sometimes on purpose. She guessed it was because he was so into growing things and constantly had plants—and the environment, too—on his brain.

Plants changed with the seasons. Like them, her brother was all about change. She was just the opposite, wanting stability despite what that dumb heart vision had said about her needing a change. She didn't!

"Why can't things just stay the same?" she murmured in an unhappy voice.

Frey ignored her complaint, bending to brush the snow off a bed of wild winterpeas. "I think this new school might be Odin's way of trying to fix the bad feelings between Vanaheim and Asgard," he went on eagerly. "If he can bring kids from all nine worlds closer together, maybe everyone everywhere will see that we can learn to get along. You and I should help with that! Come on, give peas a chance." Flashing her a grin, he turned to head down the path toward home.

"Peas?" Freya giggled, following him. His grin made it clear that the plant-related pun was no accident. But was he right? If making peas, er, peace between Asgard and Vanaheim was Odin's plan, they *should* help! Besides, that "invitation" of his was probably more like an order not to be disobeyed.

Luckily, it was her nature to look for an upside to any bad situation. Like, now she thought that if they went to Asgard, maybe someone there could tell her what had happened to Gullveig. Or explain that weird heart-shaped vision. And yet another upside occurred to her. "Well, if we really, truly do have to go, at least we can have a going-away party," she called to Frey. (Never mind that they'd just had a party to celebrate their birthday!) Her enthusiasm rose a bit as she began planning the new party in her mind. Celebrations and gatherings always raised her spirits.

"I know!" she said with excitement. "We could have it in the town square. We'll do folk dances like the *parhalling*. And for party favors I'll make—"

"Not gonna happen. We leave tomorrow," Frey informed her over his shoulder.

"Tomorrow?" Stunned by this news, Freya stopped dead in her tracks. Then she rushed ahead and turned to begin walking backward in front of him. "How can we possibly say good-bye to everyone and pack up our stuff in less than a day?"

He shrugged and moved around her. "I'm already packed. Took me five minutes. Odin said we're only allowed to bring one bag."

"*One* bag?" Freya echoed in shock.

"You should be happy, Freya. Odin chose *us*. It's an honor!"

"That's another thing. Why us?" she asked. "Don't you wonder?"

"I'm sure he had a good reason. I guess he'll tell us what it is when we get to Asgard."

Frey is too trusting, thought Freya as she turned to walk beside him. Forget any upside—she needed to talk him out of this! Because what if they found out when they got to Asgard that Odin's "invitation" was some kind of trick? That they had walked right into danger? It might be too late to return home. They'd be prisoners in enemy territory!

4
The Secret Plan

THE NEXT MORNING FREYA WOKE UP hoping that yesterday had all been a dream (or more like a nightmare, actually). But when she looked over and saw the backpack she'd filled with her stuff last night on the end of her bed, she instantly knew better. She and Frey really did have to leave home!

Then she perked up, remembering her secret plan. The one she'd brainstormed as she drifted off to sleep last night. "Mm-hmm," she murmured, nodding to herself. "Yeah, I'll go on this trip, Frey, but only to keep you out of trouble. Because you are too trusting, mister." So she'd go, all right, but as often as possible she would casually mention reasons they should turn back. Like that they'd be safer at home. But in Asgard? Who knew?

On the teeny-tiny chance her secret plan failed and she wound up stuck in Asgard, though, Freya had packed her belongings carefully. Odin's rule was one bag only. But he hadn't said how big that bag could be. Hers was ginormous! It was made of white felt and had the cutest cat faces stitched in colorful yarn all over it. She'd stuffed it with as many of her favorite outfits and keepsakes as would fit. Now it was so full, it looked like a lumpy snowman!

Pushing herself up to sit, she looked around. This house of hers and Frey's was small, like most in the village. Ever since Gullveig had left, kind neighbors had given them help when they needed it. She was going to miss them all, and her friends, too. With a sigh she flung back the covers and swung her feet to the floor.

"Eek!" The stone floor was cold as she scurried across it. She grabbed a pair of wool socks and tugged them on. After brushing the thick fall of her hair, she wove it into a single gleaming braid, leaving a few strands loose on either side. These she wove in a fancy crisscross pattern around the top of the braid at the back of her neck.

Freya glanced over at her jewel, which lay on a nearby shelf among her many necklaces. Since she wasn't holding it, it was clear now, like a diamond. "Looks like we're going on that adventure you predicted, Brising. So what should I wear?"

Brising replied in its familiar hum:

"I see you wearing black and white,
Along with something red and bright."

She considered and discarded many outfits before finally deciding on her best white linen dress. Over it she wore a shorter sleeveless red wool dress called a *hangerock* with shoulder straps that were fastened in front by tortoiseshell clasps. Her nine necklaces hung in a big, swoopy smile shape across her chest from one shoulder strap to the other.

Turning in a circle, she let her full skirt flounce. The stitched red-and-black flower border along its hem was a cheerful sight. She smiled, pleased.

"Thanks for the help, Brising. Frey thinks that choosing the perfect outfit to wear is a waste of time. But first impressions matter. The Aesir will expect the girlgoddess of love and *beauty* to be fashion forward." She wanted to look her best when meeting new people on this trip— even if some were enemies. Which anyone who lived in Asgard definitely was!

"In you go!" she trilled as she slipped Brising into its white pouch. In contact with her fingers, it briefly turned yellow green, indicating that her mood was expectant, yet uneasy or troubled. Sounded about right.

As she retied the pouch's drawstring to the gold chain necklace she wore, she heard footsteps outside. And singing? She pushed the curtain back and looked out her window. A big smile lit up her face at what she saw. Hundreds of Frey's and her friends had gathered to wish them good-bye! Word of their trip had certainly spread quickly. Thanks to Ratatosk, no doubt.

After pulling on a pair of trendy red-and-white-plaid snow boots, Freya took a last long look around, wishing she didn't have to leave so much behind. Her gaze fell on her closet, where six *hangerocks* still hung. There hadn't been room for them in her backpack.

"Hmm. That teal-and-gray one is just too amazing to leave behind." She dashed over, grabbed it, and, with much shoving, managed to get it into her pack with her other belongings. Success! She hated to leave the rest. But stuff could be replaced, she reminded herself. The hardest thing would be leaving this village behind. The people in it were as precious to her as gold.

Although it was tricky (not to mention heavy!), Freya somehow managed to sling her stuffed pack onto her back and carry it outside. A light snow was falling. In her wool socks and clothes, she hardly noticed the cold.

Frey was waiting for her, looking a lot more delighted than she was to be heading out on a new adventure. "Ready?" he asked her. She nodded, though she actually felt far from ready.

Everyone they knew had come to see them off and walked with them toward the edge of the village. Two other Vanir had been invited to attend Odin's new school—boygods named Njord and Kvasir. She and Frey had known them forever.

The yellow-haired Njord's backpack looked even lumpier and heavier than hers. "Did you pack your entire seashell collection?" brown-haired Kvasir teased him. Njord loved the seashore, and every time he visited a beach, he came back with new shells.

"Yup," Njord replied. There wasn't room for food in

their packs, but Kvasir had brought four gourds of berry juice for their trip, and he passed three of them out.

On Odin's orders, no one was allowed to accompany the departing foursome beyond the village. So when they reached the edge of town, where Freya and her three companions had to part ways with young and old friends, there were lots of hugs and good-byes.

Bye, Vana Bananas! So long, friends! Farewell, jewelry club! Vanaheim had gentle winds in summer and pretty snow in winter. *What would it be like in Asgard, the land of our enemies?* wondered Freya.

Dragging her feet, she glanced back at her family's small, cute house. It was dug partly into the ground and had bright flowers and grass growing on its roof, like most homes in the village. Would she ever see it again? Or see her many, many friends? She waved until they were specks in the distance behind her. As she walked away from all that was familiar, her hand reached to clasp the pouch that held her jewel. A few tears slid down her cheeks, but she brushed them off.

"On to Asgard!" shouted Frey, punching a fist in the air. The other two boygods did the same. Freya rolled her eyes. Maybe Frey, Njord, and Kvasir could forgive the Aesir for the war, but she *never* would.

She frowned at the rainbow winking in the morning sunlight in the far-off distance ahead of them. Even though no one in her village had ever seen it up close, everyone knew it was actually an amazing, humongous rainbow-colored bridge! Once they reached it, it would lead them to Asgard's doors.

She would do her best to convince these boys to turn back before then. Sooner or later, Brising would help her discover Gullveig's whereabouts without having to leave home forever, she told herself. And as for the heart vision . . . well . . . someone else who had far greater magical talents than she did could go help Yggdrasil if need be, right?

Freya and the three boygods walked onward,

chatting together, but they weren't alone for long. With each new path they crossed, students from other worlds joined their ranks. Kids their same age that Odin had also invited to Asgard Academy.

Frey nudged her. "Look! Light-elves." He pointed his chin toward some kids with sparkly lights woven into their hair. Everyone smiled at the sight of them—they were so happy, you just couldn't help it! They danced practically everywhere instead of walking, often joining hands in a circle, then ducking under one another's arms until they were hopelessly woven into a knot. Then they would break apart and laugh and laugh.

As the hours passed, even more students streamed in from intersecting paths, all heading for the new school. Freya had never been outside her village before and had never seen the inhabitants of any other worlds, except in art carvings at the town museum. She took note of the fascinating fashions of each group they encountered.

The dwarfs from Darkalfheim all wore colorful

caps, leather-and-gold bracelets, and pointed boots. Though they had to be about her age, they were a foot or so shorter than her and her friends.

There were humans, too, from Midgard, the middle-most of all the worlds. Their peasant costumes of woven sheep's wool were mostly vegetable-dyed in dark shades of mustard, orange, and green, but had cool special touches of colorful embroidery here and there.

"Ymir's eyebrows!" Kvasir exclaimed suddenly.

Frey and Njord whirled around, and Freya, too. "What? What's wrong?" she asked Kvasir anxiously.

But he only calmly nodded toward the humans. "Nothing. I just remembered that their world was built from Ymir's eyebrows, that's all. Makes them easy to recognize, since they all have bushy eyebrows like his."

Kvasir was a bit of a know-it-all, but he was right most of the time, like now. Ymir had been a real frost giant who'd lived in ancient times before there were any worlds at all. All nine worlds had been built upon him. *Literally.* Sky, clouds, mountains—everything had sprouted from him. From his hair, from his fingers, from you name it. Unfortunately, all the other frost giants who lived in the Jotunheim world nowadays were still kind of mad about that.

"I like their clothes," Freya said, taking a sip of juice as she studied the humans. Despite her worries about leaving Vanaheim, the idea of meeting all kinds of different students and learning about their worlds—plus getting some fashion inspiration from their clothes—was beginning to intrigue her. Not that she'd changed her mind and abandoned her go-back-home plan, mind you!

"Look! One of Yggdrasil's roots!" someone announced suddenly. At the astonishing sight of the great root, gasps of excitement and awe rippled over the crowd of students like wind over a field of wheat. The root looked as thick around as the dragon Nidhogg's tail was said to be! Freya had heard that there were only two other such World Tree roots elsewhere in the worlds.

She ran a few steps to stand on a rock so she could get a better view of the root. *Clomp! Clomp! Clomp!*

"What's that noise?" asked Kvasir.

Frey and Njord pointed at Freya.

"Huh?" she asked in surprise. "Me? What are you talking about?"

"Your boots," said Njord.

Freya looked down at them. "Oh, yeah. Sorry. They *are* kind of loud. Especially when I run." Hey, maybe this was a chance to put her secret plan into action. "Want me to go back to our village? I left another quieter pair of boots there I could change into. You should probably come with me, Frey, in case I get lost."

"Nah, the clomping's not too loud when you're only walking," said Frey. "C'mon."

"Rats!" said Freya under her breath. She'd just have to keep her eyes and ears open for another opportunity to get him to turn back.

5
Three Rings

HOURS LATER ALL THE STUDENTS PASSED through a huge broken stone wall. "What a mess!" Frey murmured, gazing around at the rubble. Although it was now a jumble of half-built sections and crumbling stone, they knew this wall had once stood tall and strong, surrounding all of Asgard. It had been destroyed just before the war ended.

Uh-oh! thought Freya. She had to wonder what kind

of reception she and the other three Vanir would get from the Aesir students with this crushed wall a constant reminder of the fighting. There wasn't much time left to convince Frey to go back home. She hadn't anticipated reaching the outskirts of Asgard so quickly.

Seeing an opening, she said to him, "Yeah, this wall used to stop giants from storming Asgard. Looks like our Vanir heroes did a lot of damage to it during the war. Now that it's broken, what's to stop the giants from attacking? Everything's going to be more dangerous for anyone living in Asgard."

"Mostly for us, since the Aesir probably still think of us as enemies," added Kvasir.

"Exactly," said Freya, pleased at his support. She'd noticed that the groups of kids from different worlds hadn't spoken to one another as they walked here. Instead groups had bunched together with their own kind, whispering and eyeing other groups with distrust.

Even now many were glancing at her and her three boy-god companions accusingly, as if thinking about the war and Vanaheim's part in it.

"If Odin thought everyone would become instant friends once he threw us together, he has another think coming," Njord noted.

Freya nodded, realizing it was true. In fact, some groups had dyed their hair all the same color to show patriotism to their worlds. Other world groups wore the same color outfits or identical badges on their clothing. Each group wanted to appear separate.

"I wonder if there will be kids from Niflheim at this school," Kvasir said from behind her.

Huh? The very thought of Niflheim, the dark, foggy world of the dead way down on the third ring, gave Freya the creeps.

"Haven't seen any so far," said Njord. He bent to pick up a seashell that had somehow found its way this far inland.

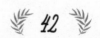

"Probably will be sooner or later," warned Freya, looking back at the boys as she carefully picked her way through the rubble. "It wouldn't be fair if Niflheim wasn't represented." But even pointing this out didn't deter Frey, who continued marching onward. Did he really not care that they might have classes with the dead? Feeling a prick of conscience, Freya turned her thoughts in a more charitable direction. If she *did* wind up having to stay at this academy, she'd try to be open-minded about the other students, dead or alive.

"I'm more worried about whether we'll meet kids from Muspelheim!" Frey declared. He and Freya had heard horrible stories about the fire giants of that world. That they burned whatever they touched. So his worry was understandable!

"Fire giants aren't allowed out of Muspelheim," Kvasir reminded them.

Still, the very idea of meeting one of them made Freya shiver even more than thoughts of meeting the dead. Back home they'd been safe. Who knew what dangers lay ahead? Why, oh, why did everything have to change?

Once the wall ruins were behind them, she, Frey, Kvasir, and Njord somehow wound up walking in the middle of the crowd of students, which Freya figured must number well over 150 by now. There were lots more students from each of the other worlds than from Vanaheim. *Why?* she wondered. Making yet another effort to persuade Frey to return home, she leaned toward him and whispered, "Hey, maybe this whole school thing isn't such a good idea. We're kind of outnumbered."

"Huh?" he said, but she could tell he wasn't really listening. Oohs and aahs had begun rippling over the group of kids, drawing his attention.

"What's going on?" wondered Kvasir.

Freya stood on tiptoe. Looking ahead, she gasped at what she saw—a huge, gleaming rainbow arch high overhead. "The Bifrost Bridge!" she announced in excitement, elbowing Frey.

"Awesome!" he replied, craning his neck to look. It had been hidden from view by Yggdrasil's branches for some time, so they hadn't realized how close they'd gotten to it.

Everyone knew that the doors to Asgard were reachable only via this magical bridge. Oh no! This meant they were almost there!

"It's not really a complete rainbow, because it has only three colors," observed a boy. He was walking alone nearby, munching some nuts from a bag he held. "The Aesir built it out of fire, air, and water. Red for fire, blue for air, and green for water."

Freya studied the dark-haired, blue-eyed boy curiously, wondering which group he belonged to. He tossed a nut high and caught it in his mouth, then grinned and wiggled his eyebrows at her. They weren't bushy, so he probably wasn't human. As if wanting to do something

45

to impress her, he pocketed the nuts and reached out toward two human girls walking ahead of him. Without their noticing, he sneakily tied together the ribbons at the ends of each of their single long braids, so that the girls were yoked together.

When one of them bent to scratch her knee, it caused a sharp tug on the braid of the other girl. "Ow!" both girls squealed. Seeing Freya staring at them as they untied themselves, they frowned at her. Did they suspect *she'd* tied their braids?

Just in case, Freya shook her head and scanned the students to find and point out the blue-eyed boy who'd done it. However, he had disappeared. When she turned back, the girls were still frowning at her over their shoulders. Before she could explain about the boy, they sped up, putting more distance between themselves and her.

"We're getting close," said Frey, speeding up a little himself and pulling her with him. "This bridge should take us all the way up to the academy."

The main entrance to Bifrost was way down in Midgard, but she could see smaller on-ramps up ahead. As they approached one of those, they passed a small sign that read BEWARE OF TROLLS.

"Why do we need to beware of them?" Freya wondered aloud.

"I heard they like to hang out under the bridge and threaten anybody who tries to cross," Kvasir informed her.

Freya was relieved to see there were no trolls in sight as students began to slow and gather around a large map. It was posted in front of the bridge on-ramp and showed how the different worlds fit together under Yggdrasil. The map showed the enormous World Tree standing in the middle of everything, with three fat rings spaced out one above the other and encircling its trunk like bracelets.

"Maybe I'm just hungry, but those three rings look like doughnuts to me," joked Njord.

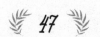

Freya, Kvasir, and Frey laughed. "Yeah. Huge doughnuts covered with worlds," said Kvasir.

"Mmm, *smultringer*," Freya murmured. *Smultringer* were among her favorite snacks. The ring-shaped doughnuts were flavored with a spice called cardamom and were best eaten warm from the frying pan. Yum!

She was getting hungry and also tired of carrying her heavy pack. They'd been walking for hours now with only berry juice to drink. Seeing fruit trees nearby, groups of students set down their bags and began picking apples and pears to snack on as everyone took turns viewing the map.

Munching a pear, Freya went to examine the map more closely too. She didn't see any heart shapes that might indicate the location of that secret new world Brising had mentioned. On the other hand, a *secret* world wouldn't be on a map! Still, the three rings seemed well-balanced as they were, with three worlds on each ring. Adding another world would upset things. It would mean ten worlds instead of a lucky nine!

The first ring—the top one—included Asgard (world of the Aesir), Vanaheim (world of the Vanir, and where Freya lived, er, *used* to live?), and Alfheim (world of the light-elves).

The second ring—the one in the middle—contained Midgard (world of the humans). To one side of that was Jotunheim (world of the frost giants), and to the other side was an underground labyrinth of tunnels and caves called Darkalfheim (world of the dwarfs).

The third ring—the bottommost one—included Niflheim (world of ice and fog, and where the good dead went to be, well, dead); Helheim (world of the evil dead ruled by a female monster); and Muspelheim (world of the fire giants), which was the most terrible world of all!

The drawing showed Yggdrasil's three enormous roots, too. One was planted in each of the three rings at the site of a spring or well from which the root could drink and nourish the World Tree. This trio of roots linked the three rings together.

"What if this whole school idea is a trick?" Kvasir commented uncertainly after they got their bags and stepped onto the bridge.

It was the same concern Freya had! Making one last desperate effort to get Frey to change his mind, she said, "Yeah, what if? It's not too late to turn back, Frey."

"Ha! You really think maybe the Aesir are planning to hold us for ransom in Asgard and make Vanaheim pay to get us back or something?" her brother scoffed.

As usual, he expected the best from everyone and was slow to get suspicious. His overly trusting nature hadn't been a worry at home in Vanaheim, where everyone they knew was a friend. But in Asgard it might put him in danger. If he was determined to keep going, she would have to go as well to look after him.

Not ready to admit defeat, however, Freya pressed

on. "It's not such a dumb idea. The goddesses and gods of Asgard are *greedy*. Everybody in Vanaheim knows that! We should get out while the getting's good."

"You're from Vanaheim?" a girl from behind them piped up.

They looked around to see that a group of about twenty-five kids their same age had stepped onto the bridge behind them. The girl who'd spoken wore her bright-white hair in two corkscrew ponytails, one on either side of her head. She was eyeing Freya, as if annoyed by her remark. Uh-oh, was this group from Asgard?

Freya nodded and smiled, trying to be friendly. "Yes we are."

"Well, look who's talking, then. Nobody's greedier than you Vanaheimers," the girl said loudly enough to reach many ears.

"Yeah! Angerboda's right!" grumbled some among her group.

Frey leaned over to Freya and quietly whispered, "I wonder what world they're from?"

"*Anger*world maybe?" Freya jokingly whispered back. Not much chance of making friends with this girl no matter what world she turned out to be from!

To Angerboda, Freya said politely, "We're *Vanir*, actually, not Vanaheimers. I'm Freya, and—"

"Well, *excuuuse* me!" Angerboda butted in. To her own pals she blared, "That troublemaking sorceress Gullveig was from Vanaheim too, remember, you guys? She stole Asgard's gold and caused a war. That's the whole reason Odin is making us go to his dumb school. So it's all these Vanaheimers' fault that the rest of us had to leave home!"

"What? That's not true!" Freya countered indignantly. "Gullveig wouldn't steal!"

But as soon as the words left her mouth, she realized she wasn't really sure of their truth. Gullveig *had* gone gold-hunting in Asgard. Had she been tempted into stealing some? Maybe the Aesir had promised to give her the gold Freya had longed for, and then tricked her out of it? Or maybe they'd treated Gullveig badly in some way that had *driven* her to steal? New determination filled Freya to find her *amma* and learn the real story. She *had* to prove this bigmouth girl wrong!

"Ha!" Angerboda grumped in disbelief. Snickers and doubting mutters sounded all around Freya and her friends now.

Uh-oh. It seemed Freya had already managed to make a bad impression on other students, at least those who'd overheard. (And also the two girls who mistakenly believed she'd tied their braids together.) Angerboda didn't even know her, but she'd obviously decided that the Vanir were all horrible and that Freya was greedy and stuck-up. This girl was loudly spreading a scrambled mix of truths and lies as fast as Ratatosk might've. She was insulting Vanaheim!

Before Freya could say something to try to correct

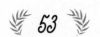

the bad impression, however, Frey got involved. "Take that back!" he said to Angerboda. He stood with his legs flexed and his fists thrust out in front of him. Njord and Kvasir immediately took similar stances on either side of him, their expressions fierce.

Ymir's knuckles! Freya thought. *Here comes trouble!*

Suddenly Angerboda and her friends magically shot up to five times their normal height. White flakes began sprinkling from their heads like dandruff. But it was actually snow!

"Frost giants!" shouted Kvasir.

"You mean Jotunheimers!" Njord joked nervously, mocking the incorrect name Angerboda had called them minutes ago.

"There's a fungus among us," Frey muttered. Another one of his nature sayings, which meant that the trouble was spreading.

When all three boys began backing away, Freya did likewise. But the giant students from Jotunheim quickly surrounded the four Vanir. Looked like this was going to turn into a fight! A very unfair one. Because there were many more giants, and they were way bigger than the Vanir right now. They could squash Freya and her companions with a few stomps of their feet!

"Calm down, Angerboda," said another girlgiant. She had long, wavy black hair, with thick streaks of white in it. For some reason she had enlarged to only half the height of the other giants. And now she shrank back down to regular size.

"A half-giant," Kvasir explained quietly to Frey, Freya, and Njord.

"Oh," Freya whispered back. That meant that only *one* of this black-and-white-haired girl's parents was a giant. She had good taste, Freya noted. The half-giant girl's feet were clad in really cool snow boots trimmed with white faux fur. (Hey, just because they were in the middle of a potential fight didn't mean she was going to stop taking note of good fashion!) Freya wanted to ask

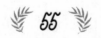

about the boots. However, now was probably not the best time, she decided.

"Butt out, Skade," Angerboda said to the black-and-white-haired half-giant girl.

Suddenly, out of nowhere, came the booming sound of stomping feet. Automatically Njord glanced over at Freya, as if suspecting she was responsible for the noise.

"I'm standing still!" she protested. "Besides, my boots aren't *that* loud!" At least she hoped not.

"Then who's stomping?" wondered Frey.

As if in reply, a boy somewhere in the crowd yelled a warning. "Fire giants! Run!"

A stampede up the bridge began as everyone, including the four Vanir, tried to escape. Freya and her brother glanced at each other with big eyes as they ran. "How did the fire giants get out?" gasped Freya. "I thought they weren't allowed to leave their world."

"Me too!" said Frey. "Maybe Odin invited them after all?"

Frost giants like Angerboda and her group were one thing. But the fire giants from Muspelheim were super scary, in view of their supposed ability to burn anything in their path.

"Ow! Ow! Hot! Hot!" yelled the frost giants, hopping from foot to foot as they ran. But when they shrank back to regular size, they stopped yelling.

For a second Freya thought the oncoming fire giants had made the bridge hot somehow. She slowed briefly enough to touch her fingertips to its surface, then continued running. "But the bridge is freezing cold!"

"It's meant to guard against trouble," mused Kvasir, who always seemed to have an explanation for everything. "When the frost giants were huge, the bridge probably sensed they were troublemakers and was trying to make them turn back from Asgard by giving them, and only them, a case of hot foot."

"So maybe it doesn't know that Odin invited them—the frost giants, I mean?" wondered Frey as they all huff-puffed their way up the bridge.

Interestingly, Skade hadn't complained about hot feet, Freya realized, dropping back behind the boys to look over at that girl as the crowd of students rushed up the bridge. Maybe that was because she was only half-giant. Or maybe it was because she wasn't a trouble-maker like some of those other frost giants!

Just then Freya caught a glimpse of that mischievous black-haired boy again. He was sitting on the bridge's golden handrail, laughing like crazy. Why wasn't he try-ing to escape like everyone else?

"Run!" she called to him in concern. But he only winked at her and stayed put. What in the nine worlds was he playing at?

6

Oops!

PUTTING THE STRANGE BOY OUT OF HER
mind, Freya didn't waste another moment as she
dashed, slipped, and slid across the Bifrost Bridge
with all the other students. *Clomp! Clomp! Swish!* Luckily, there were so many boots running now that they
drowned out the loud clomp of her own.

The bridge underfoot looked surprisingly thin and
fragile, almost like glass. She was just thinking that she
hoped it would hold them all, when someone bumped

into her from behind. Or was it an intentional shove? Her heavy backpack shifted and threw her off-balance. The bridge was so slippery that she stumbled sideways toward its handrail, losing her footing.

As Freya scrabbled for something to hang on to, her fingers got tangled in the delicate gold chain necklace that held Brising's white pouch. *Snap!* The chain broke. The pouch fell!

Trying to keep her balance, she swept an arm out to grab the pouch. She missed! *Thump.* It hit the icy bridge. "No! Brising!"

Whoosh! Her precious jewel slid from its pouch like a pea popping out of its pod. She ignored the pouch, grabbing instead for the jewel. Her teardrop jewel was boinging in a series of bounces toward the Darkalfheim end of the bridge below, back the way they'd come. Panicking, Freya dropped her backpack and fought her way through the oncoming students who were rushing in the direction of Asgard to escape a possible fire giant attack.

"Brising, come back!" She lost sight of the jewel for a while. Out of her hands, it had turned to a pale-bluish diamond that was hard to see against the icy bridge. *Wait! There it is!* She lunged for it, her fingers inches away. She touched it, and it briefly flickered all the colors of the rainbow, indicating the current state of her crazed emotions. But before she could nab it, someone's passing snow boot accidentally kicked it in a different direction. *Bonk!* It got kicked here and there by more snow boots. *Bonk! Bonk!*

And then, finally . . . *THWAP!* It was kicked upward in a high arc—up, up, up, then over the side of the bridge!

"Nooo!" Freya cried. She bent over the rail of the rainbow bridge and stretched out her hand. *Swish!* Missed again! Now she could only watch in horror as Brising sailed over the railing, to fall down, down, down toward the world of Darkalfheim.

Crack! Crack! Crack! Crack! To her astonishment, four arms broke out of the brown dirt below in that faraway

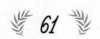

world. Gnarled hands reached up and snatched at Brising like snapping turtles. Fingers captured it before it could even hit the ground. Then the hands retreated back into the dirt as fast as they'd appeared, taking Brising with them!

The fact that the hands had come up from underground on the middle ring could mean only one thing. "Dwarfs!" she wailed. "They've got my jewel!"

Oh! If only she had replaced the gold chain that held her white pouch with something stronger. It was just that the chain had been so beautiful and she had so enjoyed wearing it. Still, how could she have been so careless? Brising was gone, and it was all her fault!

Dwarfs were always after any kind of treasure, she'd heard. Their stealing of her jewel seemed to be proof. When several student-age dwarfs rushed past her on the bridge just then, she wondered if Odin had been wise to invite them to the academy. Could they be trusted? She wasn't so sure.

By now more than half the students were beyond her, high on the bridge and moving closer to Asgard. But the rest were still coming at her from below. For a brief moment a gap opened between groups of kids, and she could see all the way down to the on-ramp where everyone had entered the bridge. Hey! There were no fire giants anywhere in sight! But there *were* big-footed trolls. They, not fire giants, were making the stomping sounds that had panicked everyone!

She wasn't scared of any ugly old troll. At least, she didn't think she was. Besides, they weren't chasing anyone. They were only jumping around on that ramp, laughing. Although they were having fun, she got the feeling they were wary of entering the bridge, for some reason. She got to her feet again and continued to move downward. Somehow she must get past them and down to Darkalfheim to rescue her jewel!

"Excuse me, sorry, excuse me!" she told everyone she bumped. The strong tide of students coming toward her kept her from gaining ground. When she stumbled and fell to her knees again, a boy wearing a turquoise tunic veered her way. Grabbing her arm, he pulled her to her feet and propelled her back *up* the bridge, *away* from Brising. It was not the way she wanted to go!

"Don't worry," he assured her as he tugged her along. "I'll help you cross to Asgard. Come on!"

"Wait! No!" She tried to pull away, but he was stronger than she was. Looking into his face, she saw that he was cute, with shaggy hair the color of hay and eyes the color of violets. "Stop! I lost something on the bridge," she insisted. "My jewel. I have to go back down for it!"

But the determined boy didn't even slow. Unfortunately, they had drawn closer to the frost giant students. Overhearing Freya, Angerboda said nastily, "Oh, boohoo. You've lost a jewel? So what? I bet you have plenty more jewels like it." The girlgiant darted an envious glance at Freya's necklaces as they ran on. "Really, you Vanir are every bit as greedy as the Aesir! Maybe even *more* greedy!"

"You don't understand . . . ," Freya told her. She blinked back tears as she stumbled along, every step taking her farther from her precious Brising.

"Whatever you lost is not worth your life! Fire giants are dangerous," her would-be, hay-haired boy rescuer told her.

"I didn't see any fire giants. Just some barefoot *trolls*, stomping around back by the entrance!" Freya informed him.

Hearing this, the boy slowed some, as did most of the students who'd overheard. Looking over their shoulders, they saw that she was indeed correct.

"Well, that's lucky!" said Frey. He'd come back for her and brought her pack, which really *was* lucky. And apparently, he'd heard everything she'd just said, because he added, "About the trolls, I mean. *Not* that you lost Brising."

"Yeah, we're safe from trolls up here," said the boy who'd been pulling her along. "They would rather lurk under the bridge than cross it. They're barefoot, and the bridge is cold!"

When Frey handed her backpack to her, the violet-eyed boy with the hay-colored hair finally released her hand and helped her shrug it on.

Suddenly she heard chattering sounds. *Ratatosk!* The gossipy squirrel was perched only a dozen feet over her head on one of Yggdrasil's low-hanging branches. Sensing a story, he peppered Freya with questions.

"You look angry. Aren't you getting along with the other students? What happened to everybody's favorite *friendly* Freya? Are you mad about having to go live with the Aesir in Asgard?" It was as if the pesky rodent could read her mind! Or part of it, anyway.

"Stop trying to make trouble!" she scolded.

"Humph! I'm a news reporter. It's my job to inquire about things. Just like your job is to respect the Aesir," said Ratatosk. "Especially now that you're going to school in Asgard!"

At this her temper flared. "I'm not bowing down to those . . ." She paused, searching for the best insult. But the only thing she could come up with was an embarrassingly childish nickname. "To those *doo-doo heads*," she finished. A hush fell over the students who'd been close enough to hear.

Ratatosk clapped his paws, looking delighted to have riled her. Grinning, he scampered off to tell the world that the Vanir goddess Freya had called the powerful Aesir of Asgard doo-doo heads.

Freya looked over at the boy who had tried to rescue her. He was frowning at her. Did that mean he was Aesir? If so, she had just insulted him big-time. *Oops!*

She opened her mouth to apologize, but Frey spoke up first. "If Brising fell off the bridge, it could be anywhere, Freya. You'll never find it again. We'll get you another jewel, though," he assured her.

"B-b-but . . . ," she sputtered. Another jewel would not be the same at all! Hers had become sort of like a beloved friend to her over time. She'd miss it terribly! Besides that, she couldn't do magic or tell the future without Brising. *It* had the magic power, not her! Unlike others in Vanaheim, she had no magic of her own. None! This was a secret she had never told anyone— not even her own brother—for fear that doing so might make everyone think less of her.

Freya didn't dare tell him now, either. The frost giants and other students would overhear. And who knew what they might do with the information? Try to take advantage of her and her friends now that her powerful jewel was gone? Or maybe try to steal Brising from the dwarfs for their own use!

The dwarfs who had taken her jewel would see that Brising was rare and beautiful. But what if they figured out it was magic, too, before she could come to its rescue? They'd never return her jewel then. Not willingly, anyway. Somehow, some way, she had to get it back before it was too late!

By now the hay-haired rescue boy had disappeared into the crowd of students waiting at the top of the bridge. She should have thanked him, even if he was Aesir. She couldn't go hunt for Brising without apologizing to him first. So when Frey urged her up the bridge, she went with him, hoping to find the boy and then quickly resume her search afterward.

As she ran higher, her snow boots clomped loudly, as usual. Startled at the sound, other students made way for her and Frey. However, she didn't see the rescue boy anywhere.

"WHO THUNDERS ACROSS MY BRIDGE?" demanded a stern voice.

Freya skidded to a halt at the top end of the bridge, but the oncoming students behind her accidentally pushed her forward. She stumbled to a stop out in front of the crowd, then looked up to find the owner of that

stern voice glaring down at her. He must be ten feet tall! Quickly she stepped backward until she blended in with the other kids again, standing next to Frey.

Dressed in an official-looking uniform, the man who'd yelled at them stood blocking their way, his thick legs planted wide. Only someone this tall, broad-shouldered, and muscular could've held such an enormous sword as the one he wielded at his side. Besides that, the biggest musical horn she'd ever seen was slung across his shoulder by a leather strap. Shaped like a ram's horn, it was made of polished gold, with etched markings decorating its length.

"Whoa! I wonder what that horn sounds like," Frey whispered to her.

"Something loud, I'm guessing," she whispered back.

Behind the formidable uniformed man were golden double doors carved with two words:

Asgard Academy

"I am Heimdall, the watchman," the man boomed. "Illustrious security guard of Asgard! Most trusted of Odin's warriors!" He paused a few seconds, as if to let that impressive news sink in. Then he went on. "I stand here day and night gazing over the worlds and guarding the Bifrost Bridge from intruders." Coming to the end of that little speech, he eyed the students suspiciously. "State your business. If you have come to cause trouble, BEGONE! Or face the wrath of my noise-toot and hurt-stick!"

"His horn and sword," Kvasir translated, though Freya had already guessed that. Heimdall obviously liked kennings, which were made-up hyphenated nick-names for things.

Before she could stop Frey from drawing attention to their little group of Vanir, he stepped forward. "None of us have come to cause trouble," he said, motioning toward the entire crowd of students around him. "We're all from different worlds, invited here by Odin to attend Asgard Academy!"

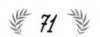

"Oh, right. I remember." Heimdall relaxed and grinned, showing off blinding-gold teeth that matched the shine of the double doors. "Welcome, students! YOU MAY PASS!"

He started to wave them all through the golden doorway. But then he called out, "Wait!" and stepped in front of it to bar their way. Stroking the tip of his long beard, he asked gruffly, "Who among you is the girl-goddess Freya?"

Freya's pale-blue eyes rounded. Before she could reply, someone gave her a small shove from behind. Looking over her shoulder, she saw it had been Angerboda. *Figures.* Freya stumbled forward a few steps.

Heimdall bent low, until they were eye-to-eye. "Freya? Vanir girl?"

"I am," she said. Her voice came out as a squeak instead of the strong tone she'd hoped to muster to impress this bossy Aesir guard.

With his sword, er, hurt-stick, he pointed to a sky-blue side door that had only just appeared. This door stood hovering in the air a few inches above the bridge, supported by nothing at all! There was a single button on it, labeled OFFICE. "You are to go to the principal's office without delay. Everyone else, proceed straight ahead through the golden portal to the academy."

"Huh?" said Freya. Did this summons have something to do with that heart-shaped vision she'd had or with her jewel's prophecy? Maybe she was about to get some explanations! She gazed at the blue door with new interest, as did everyone else. So far no one had made a move to go through either doorway. Freya leaned to one side to check behind the door and saw that it didn't seem to lead to another room or building.

"Why did the principal single out my sister? Is she in trouble?" Frey dared to ask Heimdall. At this, angry sparks flew from the guard's sword.

"Don't worry. I haven't done anything wrong," Freya warned her brother in a quiet voice. "Let's all do what Heimdall says. I'll be okay."

When she stepped forward, Frey tried to follow her. But Heimdall barred his way. "Not you. Only thunder-girl."

"Who?" asked Freya.

"I think it's a kenning he just now made up for you," Kvasir told her. "A nickname because of how you clomped up the bridge."

Freya's face warmed in embarrassment at the nickname. But she also felt relieved that Heimdall hadn't decided to call her something worse, such as clomper-girl!

As she and everyone else continued to stand there, the guard glowered at them all. "OBEY. ME. NOW!" His voice was so loud that the bridge trembled under its force.

"It'll be fine. Really. See you at the academy," Freya

assured Frey, Njord, and Kvasir. The boygods looked uncertain. However, the confident tone she'd taken on must have reassured them a little, because they didn't try to stop her as she stepped forward.

There was dead silence as she went up to the guard. When she started to pass him, Heimdall poked the tip of his sword toward her. She ducked, certain he intended to jab her with its sharp tip. Instead he slipped it under the straps of her backpack.

"Hey!" she protested as he lifted her belongings away.

"Your backpack will be taken to your pod," Heimdall informed her.

She scrunched up her nose, not understanding. "Pod?"

"Your sleep-room." He nodded at the sky-blue door. "NOW, MOVE IT! Do not keep the Great and Wonderful Odin waiting!"

"Odin? *He's* the principal?" Freya's knees wobbled

under her as her nerves gave way. But naturally he would be. This school was Odin's idea, after all. Saying nothing, Heimdall only tapped the toe of one great booted foot impatiently.

Feeling the eyes of dozens and dozens of students upon her, Freya walked over and pushed the OFFICE button. Immediately she heard music—a harp with the notes sliding upward in a pretty melody. Then the blue door swung open.

She stepped through it. And suddenly she was falling . . . *UP!*

7
Odin

Topsy-turvy, skirts and hair flying, Freya found herself whisked head over heels, up, up, and away through the longest vine slide she'd ever encountered. It was totally fun, with spirals and loop-the-loops galore! Good thing Heimdall had taken her backpack, though, or everything would have spilled out and whooshed around her in here like a tornado.

Minutes later she shot out of the end of the vine and somersaulted to a sudden stop with hopelessly tangled hair hanging in her face. "Wow! I've never fallen up before! Where am I?" she asked herself, breathlessly finger-combing her glittery hair out of the way. "Ymir's eyeballs!" she whispered in awe once she could see properly. She was straddling one of the highest branches of Yggdrasil like it was a horse! From here she could look down on . . . *everything*.

With one hand locked on either side of the branch she'd landed on, Freya struggled to keep from falling off. She could see all three rings and parts of all nine worlds far below, including her own, Vanaheim. Everyone down there was too small to make out, so she couldn't recognize her friends or even her house from this distance. She could see Bifrost down there too. At its highest end, it looked as if it had been invaded by tiny ants. No, those must be Frey and the other students moving across the bridge and through the double gold doors!

Such quick, lengthy upward travel as she'd done in so short a time seemed impossible. Still, Odin was the most powerful god in all the worlds. He could probably make practically *anything* happen.

Just then two black ravens swooped past, startling Freya into falling off her perch. Next thing she knew, she was tumbling down to land upon another, much larger branch directly below the one she'd been sitting on. *Oomph!* This lower branch was wider than two houses and worn flat on top by many footsteps. Luckily, it was also covered with a bed of soft ferns that cushioned her landing.

"Hey, you made me fall!" she scolded the ravens.

"*Caw*fully sorry!" one *caw*led, er, called.

"That's be*caws* we didn't see you till it was too late," added the other.

Cool! She'd never heard birds speak in a way she could actually understand. Their language seemed to be a blend of hers and theirs, the latter of which was basically, well, lots of caws. They flew on, disappearing over a square horizontal platform fifty feet or so away.

About as wide as her house in Vanaheim, it rested high above her upon a nest of woven branches.

Hearing voices coming from atop the platform, Freya stood and made her way along the path that led up to it. The fernway soon turned into a smaller path paved with stones. Ankle-breakers, Heimdall would likely call them, because the uneven stones were jumbled every which way and you had to walk carefully to avoid tripping. It was as if whatever or whoever was at the top of that platform didn't want visitors.

Finally Freya reached a ladder and began climbing. She counted ninety-nine rungs before she finally got to the top. Once she stood on the platform, she gasped at its beauty. Gleaming silver branches twined upward from its back and sides, weaving together to form three fancy decorative walls and a partial roof. It looked sort of like a huge and magnificent, but incomplete, birdcage. At the partially covered platform's far side were two thrones, upon which sat a man and a woman, both wearing crowns.

"Come!" the man bellowed. His deep, authoritative voice made Freya jump to obey. As she approached, she noticed that the thrones were alive! Their seat backs were made of gnarled ash-wood branches with leaves that were constantly budding out, turning green, then yellow, then bright shades of red and purple, all within a few seconds. After reaching that final color, the leaves would drop off to wither on the floor around the thrones and be blown away by a constant whipping wind.

The man who'd shouted wore a splendid blue cloak. And the two black ravens that had startled her before now sat on each of his shoulders, while two gray wolves napped at his feet. There was a black patch over one of his eyes. His other eye—a clear, intelligent blue one— was fixed on her.

This had to be Odin! If she'd had any doubt of

this, the runeword carved on the high back of his chair would've erased it. It spelled HLIDSKJALF, which everyone knew was the name of his throne.

"Come, Freya!" he called, motioning her closer. He knew her name? Oh, of course he would. He'd told Heimdall to send her here to his office!

The platform's floor was also made of stones, but these were set evenly and engraved with mysterious runes. She clomped across them to reach Odin.

On the throne next to his sat a woman with a single long blond braid hanging forward over one shoulder. A spinning wheel stood before her, upon which she was spinning long threads of white wool to form a large, puffy-fluffy bubble that was bobbing in the air above her head. At Freya's approach, she cut the thread, which caused the entire bubble to drift upward through the open roof. Freya watched it float out into the sky to join other similar objects. *Whoa!* This woman was spinning real, actual clouds!

The woman gazed curiously at the necklaces Freya wore, her eyes coming to rest on the broken gold chain that had once held Brising. Freya's fingers were nervously toying with the chain's halves, which still dangled from the shoulder straps of her dress. Quickly she tied the chain ends together and let her hands drop to her sides.

"*Velkommen* to Valaskjalf," the woman said finally, a greeting of welcome.

Wow! This is Valaskjalf? Freya viewed it with new wonder. Rumor had it that from this place Odin observed everything that happened in all nine worlds!

"I'm Ms. Frigg. I'm coprincipal of Asgard Academy with my husband, Odin," the woman went on. "What's your favorite color?"

"Huh? Well, red, I guess," Freya replied, wondering why she'd asked. Immediately Ms. Frigg reached into a bag beside her throne. She pulled out a ball of red yarn with knitting needles stuck into it and began knitting.

Odin leaned forward. "You are the girlgoddess Freya, correct?"

Freya nodded.

"I hear that you possess a wonderful skill? And can do magic?" His one good eye gazed at her with interest.

Gulp. This was not her favorite topic at the moment. "All the Vanir can do some kind of magic. I'm not special in that way," she replied truthfully. The fact was she couldn't do any magic at all without her jewel, and she'd lost that. She thought it best not to share this information, however, at least not before she found out what he expected of her.

To her surprise, Odin chuckled. "Oh, we think you *are* special."

Wrong! she thought. But she didn't say so out loud.

"Frigg and I wouldn't have brought you to our new school if you weren't," he went on seriously. "We were wary of bringing more Vanir to Asgard Academy right away, since our two worlds have been at war. We'll see how things go with you and the three boygods first."

"Um. Okay." Nothing like putting pressure on Frey, Njord, Kvasir, and her to do well at AA. And to behave themselves! Would Odin expel her once he found out she had no magic without Brising, though? If she failed to meet his expectations—or bailed and went home—it sounded like it was going to hurt the chances of other Vanir being invited to enroll here in the future, she realized guiltily.

Odin glanced at the raven on his left shoulder. "Well, what do you think of her, Munin?" he asked it. After it cawed a few times in his ear, he looked at the raven on his right shoulder. "And you, Hugin?" That one caw-answered in his other ear. The ravens weren't speaking in a way she could understand now, which must mean they didn't want her to know what they were saying.

"Hmm." Appearing to think over their replies, Odin lifted a juice glass at his side and drank from it. Then, for no reason at all, he drifted off into reciting poetry! He said:

"Breaking branch, or flaring flame,

Freya of all-seeing fame,

Welcome to my throne and hall.

Have you come to fix our . . . ?"

Frowning, he eyed her as if expecting her to supply the word he sought for his poem.

"Um, snowball? Waterfall? Heimdall?" she guessed.

After each suggestion he shook his head. Seeming a little disappointed in her, he finally said, "Never mind."

Well, if he'd wanted a poet, why had he called upon her? She'd never been any good at poetry. Nor had she ever claimed to be. Besides, she hadn't come here to fix anything. And Odin was mistaken if he thought she was a seer of great fame!

Seizing the opportunity that his current silence provided, Freya opened her mouth and burst out with her biggest burning question. "Can you please tell me where my *amma* Gullveig is?"

At this, Odin's frown deepened. In a voice she had to strain to hear, he murmured, "I only wish I knew."

"I thought you could see, er, that you know everything," she said in surprise. (Obviously, he didn't, or else he would know all her secrets, like the fact that she lacked magical talent now that she'd lost Brising!)

Odin raised an eyebrow. "As you must know yourself, seers can't actually *see everything*. And what they can see is not always easily understood."

"Gullveig did come here, though, right?" she persisted.

"And started a war between Asgard and Vanaheim!" Odin pounded his fist on the arm of his throne. He looked so annoyed that Freya didn't dare mention Gullveig again.

Then he sighed. "A war that neither side could win. Yggdrasil doesn't do well when there's fighting. Not well at all. Thing is, the future of all our worlds hangs on that tree's welfare. It provides a link between the rings, shelter from storms, homes for animals, wood for

building, the list goes on and on." He spread his arms wide and gazed out at the leafy tree with deep respect.

"If we destroy that *caw*some tree . . . ," Hugin began.

"We *caw*se our own destruction," finished Munin.

Odin slowly nodded. "Another war could mean *caw*tastrophe, er, catastrophe!"

Was Odin saying what she thought he was saying? That if those who lived in the nine worlds could not get along, the World Tree would sicken? Maybe even die? She remembered Frey pointing out that the plants in Vanaheim got droopy during the war. If Yggdrasil and the plants all died, would that cause those who lived in the worlds to die too? This was a new idea to her. And it *changed* everything!

As if noting her dismay, Odin went on. "Ah, you begin to understand the responsibilities of your position here."

"Fear not, however," Ms. Frigg put in. "With your exceptional talent, you will undoubtedly be a big help in uniting the nine worlds."

Odin nodded. "Tell me, how does it work for you? Your future-telling magic, I mean."

"Oh! Um, I use a jewel," Freya said honestly.

Odin sat up straighter, his eye gleaming with interest. "Show me."

This leader of the Asgard gods was both admired and feared for his ability to see into all the worlds at once. She would love to know how he accomplished that. Anyway, he had already admitted that he couldn't see absolutely everything everywhere all the time. He hadn't seen her lose her jewel on the bridge. Or maybe he had but just didn't realize it was that particular jewel that gave her seeing abilities?

Would he banish her back to Vanaheim if he found out she wasn't valuable as either a seer *or* a poet? Finding Gullveig and discovering where those dwarfs had taken her jewel likely depended on her being able to stay here long enough to do some detective work!

Only then remembering that she had forgotten her

jewel's white pouch back on the bridge, she lifted a hand and grasped the pouch that contained the kittycart marble instead. She would pretend Brising was inside it! Crossing the fingers of her other hand, she hoped Odin couldn't see through the pouch and figure out she was about to tell a lie. But before she could open her mouth to speak, Odin asked, "Don't you need to take your jewel out for it to work?"

Nervously she blurted, "My jewel is shy, so I'm letting it stay in its pouch."

Odin raised an eyebrow, but he didn't question what she'd said.

Phew! Freya closed her eyes and pretended to get a vision right away. "I see a heart." She was describing what she'd seen back at Gullveig's hut, of course. Through her eyelashes she watched for Odin's reaction.

"Tell me more," he instructed. He gave no sign as to whether he already knew about that wooden heart or was simply interested in her vision.

Argh! She'd been hoping that *he* might give *her* a clue as to what that whole heart business was about. She decided to share one last tidbit. "Oh, and I see something about a so-called secret world?"

Instantly he straightened. His eye intensified to an even brighter blue. "Hmm," he said, tapping his chin with two fingers. "A heart? A secret world? But that's nonsense!" Her eyes widened as he half rose from his throne, shouting, "What I'd like you to see in your visions is the whereabouts of that gold thief, Gullveig!"

Startled, Freya took a step backward. It seemed that Odin believed Gullveig had stolen Asgard's gold too! Did he have proof, though, or had he only heard the rumors? Just then a horn sounded. It was so loud, it caused vibrations that made the platform and everything on it shake. Freya gasped. "Was that Heimdall's horn?"

In an instant Odin's anger seemed to vanish. Chuckling, he plopped back in his throne. "Don't worry. It's only one blast. But if you ever hear five hundred and forty of them, get ready for real trouble. Doomsday!"

"Doomsday?" Freya echoed in horror. That word again. Just like in Brising's future-telling yesterday!

At Freya's frightened tone Ms. Frigg set down her knitting. She put a hand on Odin's arm, which caused him to shrug and fall silent on that subject. Now he lapsed into rhyme once more:

> "At many a feast I arrived too late,
> Though much too soon at some;
> Go eat hearty and make new friends,
> Or thin you will . . ."

He paused, as if trying to come up with a rhyme for "some." For once a rhyming word leaped to Freya's mind, but she was reluctant to say it after failing to supply the correct word to Odin's previous poem. Ms. Frigg lifted her eyes from her knitting and nodded at her, as if guessing that Freya had a suggestion and urging her to speak.

"Become?" Freya ventured after several seconds.

Odin clapped his hands in delight. "Yes! The rhyming word is 'become.' *Or thin you will become.* One of my better poems, if I do say so myself," he said, praising his own cleverness.

He turned to Munin. "Remember that one," he told the bird.

As the raven nodded, Freya suddenly recalled that *munin* meant "memory." So did this bird memorize all of Odin's poems as a permanent record?

"Heimdall has sounded the dinner horn. You must be hungry," Ms. Frigg said to Freya. "I imagine you missed lunch on your journey here?"

"Well, yes," Freya replied. "We had some apples and pears along the way, but there wasn't room for food in our packs."

Odin sat back in his chair and jerked his chin to indicate that she could go now. How did he do that— manage to make a mere nod of his head look so regal?

"We will talk again another time," he informed her.

"Yes, off with you to the Valhallateria," said Ms. Frigg, smiling.

Val-hall-uh-TEER-ee-uh. Freya repeated the long word in her mind. It was a mouthful. Whatever a Valhallateria was, she would rather be there than stay here a minute longer under Odin's all-seeing eyeball. Plus, it sounded like there would be food there. Maybe even *smultringer*!

Eager to comply with Ms. Frigg's gentle order, she spun around, ready to head for the ladder. But that wouldn't take her all the way to the school, so . . . Pausing, she sent a questioning look over her shoulder at her hosts. "Um, how do I get there?"

Having picked up her knitting again, Ms. Frigg pointed a knitting needle toward the empty space beyond Freya. Instantly the blue door reappeared. "Go on. Through that portal," Ms. Frigg instructed.

"Thanks," Freya said gratefully.

94

Odin was still eyeing her. Somewhat suspiciously, she thought. It kind of made her want to come clean about her shortcomings. Yet she couldn't quite bring herself to admit the truth—that she now possessed no more magic than a Midgard human. Which meant no magic at all!

What would Odin do when he discovered she couldn't meet his (extremely high!) expectations of her? she wondered as she headed for the blue door. Maybe instead of just sending her back home, he'd toss her off a high branch like a sack of leaves! She shuddered at the thought. Somehow she had to get her jewel back before he figured things out. And before the dwarfs who had stolen Brising discovered its magic power. Because not only would they never give it back then. They'd keep it to use themselves!

8

Brising

MEANWHILE, DEEP DOWN IN THE WORLD of Darkalfheim, the gnarled hand that had caught Freya's jewel withdrew under the earth into a dim tunnel. "Oho! Lookee what we got here," said the greedy voice of a dwarf named Alfrigg.

A trio of other dwarfs, all holding torches, crowded around to admire the teardrop jewel. Lit by the torchlight, it glittered in Alfrigg's palm. "It's clear. Must be a diamond!" he said.

"WHAT DID HE SAY?" asked Berling. After years of banging hammers in the mines, he didn't hear very well.

"He said 'DIAMOND'!" Dvalin yelled into Berling's ear.

"Grabbers keepers! Losers weepers!" A dwarf named Grerr grabbed the jewel from Alfrigg and ran off with it, laughing. "This diamond is perfect for that new necklace we're making. And since I've got it now, I should get to design its setting!"

The other three dwarfs dashed through the tunnel after him. "Give it back!" Alfrigg grumped. As the four-some turned down another tunnel—one among many in an underground labyrinth of caves—Alfrigg man-aged to snatch back his sparkly prize. He and Grerr began fighting loudly over it.

"Shush!" Dvalin warned. "Odin may have only one eye, but he can see just about any place with it if he knows where to look. If he learns what we've found, he might take it from us."

All four dwarfs hunched their shoulders and studied their surroundings as if spies might be listening. "He can't see down here in the tunnels," scoffed Alfrigg. But he spoke in a hushed whisper, appearing a little worried.

"Just in case, let's skedaddle," Grerr suggested.

"WHAT?" asked Berling.

"HE SAID, 'LET'S SKEDADDLE'!" yelled Dvalin.

"Hey, I thought you said to stop yelling," complained Grerr.

"WHAT?" asked Berling.

Alfrigg rolled his eyes and thrust Freya's jewel inside his knapsack. When he took off running, the other three followed. The dwarfs wound down, down, down, deep into the earth, till eventually they reached their workshop.

9

Valhallateria

FREYA STUDIED THE BLUE DOOR THAT HOVERED
before her, her back turned to Odin's and Ms. Frigg's
thrones. Several rows of buttons had popped up on the
door this time, each labeled with a place name, such
as Vingolf, Breidablik, Gladsheim, and Valhallateria. It
seemed that from this office you could go anywhere in
Asgard Academy!

She pressed the button labeled VALHALLATERIA.
Immediately she heard that harp sound as the blue

door opened. However, she wasn't instantly sucked up through a vine, as she had been back at the Bifrost Bridge. Instead, after pushing through the door, she stepped straight into a grove of amazingly beautiful trees clad in fluttering red-gold leaves. Wow!

Snick! The blue door shut behind her and disappeared again. Now there was no way to get back to the office. Perhaps the blue door became visible only when Odin or Ms. Frigg wanted to transport you—or themselves—somewhere.

As she wound through the trees along a path, Freya heard the horn blast again and quickly covered her ears to muffle the sound. Heimdall's second dinner call, no doubt. Hearing voices ahead and glimpsing her brother, she hurried to catch up with him. To her surprise, he was walking with three other boygods she didn't know, and they were all talking away as if they were already buds. She silently trailed them, listening in.

"You know that mythical flaming sword? The one

called Firebrand?" one of the boys was asking. He had brown curly hair and was holding a musical instrument called a lute.

The others nodded. "By Odin's might, one day it will be mine!" declared a red-haired boy. He was taller and more muscular than the other boys.

Another boygod with black hair and dark-blue eyes started laughing. "You wish! You'll never get that sword." Freya recognized him. It was that boy from the bridge who had tied the girls' braids together!

"Will too, or my name isn't Thor, the destined-to-be greatest warrior of all time!" the red-haired boy proclaimed loudly.

"Freya! Hey! What happened with Odin?" her brother called out when he noticed her.

She caught up with him then, and they all five kept walking. No way was she going to tell Frey the details of her visit to Valaskjalf with his new friends listening in, though.

"Oh, he just had a few questions about Vanaheim," she answered casually. "No big deal." She frowned at the black-haired, blue-eyed boy from the bridge.

"I'm Loki," he said. Slouching a little, he flipped his hair, acting all cool. He was snacking again, this time on a pear he must've gotten from that orchard back near the bridge. It reminded her of how hungry she was.

"Bragi," the boy with the lute told her, grinning good-naturedly.

"Thor," said the red-haired boy, though she'd already heard his name, of course.

"I'm Frey's sister," she told them, knowing they must have guessed that. She smiled at them, and they all looked a little dazzled. She was used to having that effect, though. She was the girlgoddess of love and *beauty*, after all!

"So . . . ," Frey began, and she knew he was going to ask about Odin again.

"Aren't these the most beautiful trees in all the

worlds?" she asked, gazing at their surroundings, before he could go on. As she expected, talk of growing things sparked his enthusiasm, and he began remarking on the kinds of trees they were passing.

"Yeah! See those rowan trees with the red berries?" said Frey. "Beautiful specimens. And those spruces over there are the tallest and bluest I've ever seen." Then he gestured toward the forest floor, pointing out flowers, such as the purple harebells that were growing alongside bilberry and holly bushes.

"I like those," said Bragi, pointing at the red-gold trees.

Freya nodded. "Me too. Their leaves make a pretty fluttering sound in the wind."

"They're aspen trees. Their wood is lightweight. Great for shield making," Frey informed them.

"Good to know," said Thor. "I could use a new shield."

They were very close to the trunk of the great ash tree Yggdrasil now, Freya saw. This entire forest grew atop a single one of the World Tree's vast branches, which had to be hundreds of feet across and who knew how long!

Soon they entered a grove of thin birch trees growing close together, and so had to walk single file to thread through them. Freya fell back a bit, wanting to enjoy the quiet. Once through the birches, they came right up alongside Yggdrasil's trunk.

Ymir's freckles! How fantastic is this! Glancing ahead, Freya saw that the boys had rounded a bend in the path and moved out of sight. Did she dare? Yes! She did. She stepped toward Yggdrasil's enormous trunk, close enough to smell the fresh outdoorsiness of its sap. Reaching out, she brushed her palm across its bark. Wait till she told her friends back in Vanaheim that she had actually touched the trunk of the most famous tree in all the nine worlds!

Ka-chunk! The section of bark she'd touched jerked to one side. A small opening appeared on a level with her face—a little viewing window about ten inches wide and three inches tall.

She jumped back in surprise. Abruptly an eye (brown like the one in that heart vision Brising had shown her) appeared in the small open slot. *Weird!* She stumbled back a few more steps. She hadn't thought anyone lived inside Yggdrasil's trunk. Except maybe burrowing bugs or a raccoon family. But this was no bug or raccoon eye.

"Who's there?" Freya demanded. The eye blinked, but before whoever it belonged to could reply, she heard Frey's faraway voice calling her name. The little window slid shut with a thump.

"Wait!" She leaped forward and knocked at the place where the window had been, but it didn't reappear. In fact, there wasn't any sign it had ever existed! "Open up!" she shouted, tapping on the bark again. No response.

Hey! What's that delicious smell? Her attention suddenly drawn away from the tree trunk, she sniffed the air hungrily. *Food!* She was starving! Abandoning the tree mystery for now, she hurried to catch up with the boys. They were entering a large building with a sparkling gold-thatched roof when she spotted them. A few seconds later she pulled on the V-shaped door handles and followed them inside.

It turned out that the Valhallateria was basically a school cafeteria. But it was nothing like the one at her old school. Sure, this cafeteria was filled with tables and chairs. However, these had legs made out of bent metal spears! Plus, the chairs' backs and seats were formed from two thick wooden shields set at right angles. The superhigh ceiling was tiled with hundreds more shields and spears of her very favorite metal— shiny, dazzling gold!

Not only that, but all around her the walls were covered with fantastic wooden friezes, which were basically huge sculpted paintings done in bright colors. The carved scenes showed hundreds of heroic-looking warriors feasting and marching. Awesome!

But now something else amazing caught her eye: a larger-than-life, goat-shaped ceramic fountain standing on a table in the middle of the room. Talk about unusual! Fascinated, she went over to study it. Circling the fountain, she noticed that the table it stood upon had a pedestal shaped like a stout tree trunk and green-painted leaves that formed a flat, rectangular tabletop. Sparkly water poured out of spigots on all sides of the goat into a trough.

Freya scanned the big room for her brother, wanting to show it to him. However, he and his new buddies had already joined Njord and Kvasir to sit at a big table across the room. She was glad Frey was meeting other students so quickly. Still, it made her feel a little left out. For some reason she had expected her brother to need her help in making new friends at this academy, but she'd obviously been wrong about that.

She had always had an easy time making friends of her own, but because of the trip to Odin's office, she hadn't yet had a chance to. Well, she was going to work on that right now. Even if she wasn't planning to stay long, she would like to leave behind a better impression than she had made so far!

Spying the hay-haired boygod in the turquoise tunic who'd helped her on the bridge, she went over to him. "Hi. I'm Freya," she announced brightly.

The boy's cheeks flushed and he stuffed his hands into his pockets. "Yeah, I know."

Loki had left the table where he'd been sitting with Frey and his other companions. Coming up to Freya, he nodded toward the boy. "He's odd."

"That's not a very nice thing to say," scolded Freya.

The cute, hay-haired boy's cheeks flushed a little. "That's my name, he means. It's Od."

"Told you," Loki said to Freya, grinning mischievously.

"Oh," said Freya, finally getting it. "So anyway . . . Od," she began as Loki continued to hang around, "thanks for what you did on the bridge. Helping me not to get trampled."

Od flushed again, seeming shy now that they weren't in danger. Keeping his hands in his pockets, he mumbled, "Sure. No problem."

"Come on, Od," Loki butted in, "when a girl comes over to talk, you should talk!" He turned to face Freya. "Od and I are both from Asgard. We're Aesir, your used-to-be enemies."

"Oh really?" Freya said, stiffening. So she'd guessed right about Od being an Aesir. She supposed all of Frey's new guy friends were too, since they'd all been hanging out with Loki.

Od nodded. "Yeah, we just went down the bridge today to see if we could help all you new kids coming to the school."

"You did help! Me, anyway," she said earnestly.

"On the bridge you said you don't like Aesir, though, right?" Loki prodded.

Od looked at her in surprise.

"Sorry about that," she told them politely. "I was just, um, in a bad mood."

"It's not easy having to start at a new school," Od said with a small, kind smile. "Most of Loki's and my friends are still going to our old school, Asgard Junior High, but Odin sent us here." He had this interesting way of cocking his head while he talked, so that he looked up at you from an angle. And that smile of his was cutely crooked. He'd been sweet to her back on the bridge. Maybe she could help him out in return by chatting with him a bit now. From what Loki had said, she guessed Od was only shy around girls.

"So what was your old school like?" she asked. But before he could answer, Angerboda walked by.

Rolling her eyes, the girlgiant gave a snort. "You again! I was hoping Odin would send you back to Vanaheim, where you belong!"

Od blinked, obviously startled by Angerboda's outburst but unsure how to react. *What was it with this girl, anyway?* wondered Freya. Angerboda seemed to have taken an immediate dislike to her!

Loki grinned. "Not me. I'm glad you're both here. We could use some new kids in Asgard." He flicked his eyes toward Od. "Right, buddy?" Loki elbowed Od, then winked at Freya and Angerboda.

To Freya's surprise, Angerboda blushed and sent Loki a sweet, hopeful smile. Then, looking all flustered, she hurried away. *Hmm. Interesting reaction.*

Od shifted from one foot to the other, drawing Freya's attention. "Well, guess I'll see you around," he said to her. Then, just like Angerboda, he walked off without another word.

"He likes you," Loki declared as Freya watched Od head across the room.

"What?" This was the last thing she had expected him to say. Was it true? Od wasn't acting like he liked her, in her opinion. And as the girlgoddess of *love* and beauty, she could usually tell when a boy liked a girl and vice versa.

For instance, she had a feeling Angerboda was crushing on the very boy who still stood before her—*Loki*! Unfortunately, it was harder to judge crushing when it came to herself. Her powers didn't help her much then. Anyway, she had never *like*-liked any boy before and wasn't about to start now, even if one did like her. She had way more important stuff to worry about. Like getting her jewel back!

Frowning at Loki, Freya changed the subject. "You're the boy who tied those girls' braids together."

"Yeah, hilarious, right?" Loki laughed merrily. He had a charming face and a grin that made you want to laugh along with him, but she held back. What he'd done was mean! "And how'd you like my joke about the fire giants being on the bridge?" he added.

"What? You were the one who shouted that? Knowing it wasn't true?" Freya said, taken aback.

"Hey, it was just a little Loki jokey," he replied. His grin only infuriated her more.

She shook her head. "First of all, the braid thing was *not* funny. And neither was the fire giant thing. That stampede made me drop my magic j—um, my backpack." If she wasn't going to tell Odin about losing Brising, she certainly shouldn't tell this boy. Someone who would do the mean tricks he'd done wasn't trustworthy.

"Apple juice, anyone? Made it myself," said a hopeful voice. A sweet-faced girl with apple-red cheeks had come over. She gestured to the large ceramic goat fountain in the middle of the room. Apparently, it was spouting juice, not water.

Freya turned toward the girl. "Juice sounds perfect. I'm really thirsty. And starving!" Abandoning Loki, she followed the girl over to the fountain, adding, "I'm Freya."

The girl smiled. "I'm Idun." She pointed at the goat. "And this is Heidrun."

This big ceramic goat fountain has a name? The idea

made Freya smile too. Among the leaves on its tree-top table were stacks of green glass *hrimkalder*—short cups with rounded bottoms. Drinking horns too. Freya picked up one of the *hrimkalder* and held it beneath a spigot.

Once her cup was half-full, she took a sip. "Mmm! This is the best apple juice I've ever tasted," she complimented Idun honestly.

"Plus, it will make you stay forever young," said a new voice. That half-giant girl named Skade—the one with the cool faux-fur snow boots—had come over. She wasn't half-giant size right now, though, just regular, same as Freya and Idun.

"Immortal, you mean?" Freya asked, looking from Skade to Idun in surprise. Where she came from, goddesses and gods didn't live forever. She'd thought that was true for the Aesir, too.

"Not immortal, but we'll all stay our same age if we keep drinking this juice. Right, Idun?" said Skade, taking a sip from the drinking horn she held. Idun nodded.

"Awesome!" said Freya. She reached for another cupful.

Beyond the goat she suddenly noticed a small glass dome affixed to a tall, square wooden column. There was a large button under it labeled with the words:

X540

Push only

in the event

of Ragnarok

Freya stared at the button curiously. What was Ragnarok? And what would this button do if you broke the glass and pushed it?

She was about to ask Idun or Skade if they knew, when—*wham!*—two swinging doors in the wall beyond the column banged open, revealing a glimpse into the Valhallateria's kitchen.

A dozen cafeteria ladies with big muscles swarmed out of the doors to circulate among the tables. Each carried a six-foot-wide tray, balanced on one hand, that held many steaming plates of food. *Finally—dinner!*

"Everyone! Sit! Time to eat!" the servers commanded in boisterous song. They sounded like loud opera singers harmonizing! Each wore a gleaming metal helmet that resembled an upside-down bowl with a tall wing on either side and a carved *V* in front. Across their chests they wore breastplates with rows of loops down the front that held silver spoons and knives and fresh rolled-up napkins. *Whoosh!* Large wings sprouted from their backs. The armor-wearing ladies lifted off to fly in different directions a foot or so above the ground and pass out the food.

"Valkyries," Freya heard other students murmur. So that's what these cafeteria ladies were called.

"Quick. Let's sit here," she suggested to Skade and Idun as the servers got busy setting places at tables and handing out plates of food with military efficiency and precision.

The minute the three girls sat, a Valkyrie plunked down yummy-smelling food and silverware for them. The hungry girls dug in, chatting between bites at Freya's prompting. "So, you're a giant?" she ventured to Skade to get the conversation going.

"Half-giant," said Skade, confirming Freya's guess back on the bridge. "My mom's Aesir, though. So growing up, I spent the school year in Asgard, but summers in Jotunheim with my dad."

Since Skade was part Aesir, that meant she was a former enemy of Vanaheim too! Or at least a *half* enemy. But she was also part frost giant, and didn't those giants dislike absolutely anyone who wasn't from Jotunheim because of what had happened to Ymir long ago?

Old feelings of distrust toward Asgard and Jotunheim collided with Freya's positive feelings for these two girls, who seemed super nice. Confused, she sat back in her chair and let Skade and Idun do the talking as she ate. Her platter contained a bowl of wild plums, cherries, and hazelnuts, and skewers of hot roasted meat and veggies, alongside buttered bread with honey and cheese.

These were the same kinds of foods she'd eaten back in her village. However, they didn't taste quite the same. They were spiced differently. Although she wasn't sure she liked the change, she was so hungry, she scarfed it all down anyway.

When Skade and Idun finished eating, they bid Freya good-bye, as they had been called over to visit with friends seated elsewhere in the Valhallateria. Freya remained behind, still eating. As she polished off the last crumb on her plate, she noticed that the servers had lined up in front of those sculpted paintings, arms crossed and eyes watchful.

"Hmm. I wonder why the Valkyries are guarding the friezes on those walls?" she murmured to herself. At least, that was what they *appeared* to be doing.

"Here she is," a voice remarked. Loki! He'd come back. And he had steered another student—a thin boy with dark, shaggy hair—over to her table to meet her. Having introduced them (sort of), Loki stood back, smirking as if expecting some drama to unfold between the boy and her.

10
The Deal

*U*H-OH, THOUGHT FREYA. THE SHAGGY-HAIRED
student standing next to Loki was staring at her with a
big, goofy, liking sort of smile on his face.

"Hi, uh, Freya?" the shaggy boy said to her. His fingers fiddled with a leather cord around his neck, from
which dangled a miniature carved wooden horse painted
brown with white spots.

She nodded at him uncertainly. "Yes, that's me."

He didn't look at all familiar. He had bushy eyebrows. A human?

"Did you get my letter?" the boy asked eagerly. "I was just wondering because you didn't answer it."

"Um . . . ," said Freya, trying to remember. She got lots of mail asking for advice about crushes. They usually began, "Dear Girlgoddess of Love." She always answered them, but it could take a while if she was busy with schoolwork or her clubs. "I'm sorry. I get so many letters. Sometimes I get behind in replying," she replied kindly.

Beside her she heard Loki snicker. Did he think she had gotten this boy's letter but had been too lazy to answer or something? *Humph.* No way! She decided to ignore him.

"What's your name?" she asked the shaggy-haired boy.

"Mason," he replied. He gestured at the tiny horse on the cord around his neck, adding, "And this is Unlucky."

Freya cocked her head. Since she had named her jewel Brising, it didn't surprise her that he'd given a name to the horse on his cord. Still, Unlucky seemed a strange choice. "Mason, huh?" The boy's name did ring a bell. *Had* she read his letter? She thought hard, trying to recall.

Mason went on. "I'm worried about you."

"What? Why?" asked Freya.

The boy stepped closer and warned, "This place is dangerous. The wall around Asgard was partially destroyed in the war. It needs to be rebuilt to keep you safe from—"

"Dastardly frost giants?" Loki finished for him.

Mason frowned at him. "I was going to say 'trouble-makers.'" Then, looking besotted again, he put his hands over his heart and went down on one knee before Freya. "I offer to rebuild the wall. For you."

"For me?" she squeaked in surprise. This boy was definitely crushing on her. Whenever this kind of thing happened, she tried not to hurt a boy's feelings. She usually wrote back and gently guided his attention to other girls by giving him tips on how to meet them. She wished she'd gotten his letter and replied, but he seemed so determined that she doubted he'd have taken such advice anyway. He appeared smitten with her—or, more likely, some perfect image of her he had conjured up inside his head.

"That's a really sweet offer, Mason. We saw the wall rubble on the way here. But don't work on rebuilding the wall just for me. Do it for the good of our nine worlds, and Yggdrasil, too," she urged. "By safeguarding Asgard *and* the World Tree, you'll be helping us all."

But instead of following her suggestion, Mason climbed to stand atop her table. "I give my heart to Freya!" he shouted. "I will rebuild Asgard's wall to protect her, if only she will give me *her* heart in return, plus the sun and the moon!"

"Hush! Get down," she pleaded, leaping up and flapping her hands at him in embarrassment.

123

Meanwhile, Loki was cracking up. "Ha-ha-ha! Dude, you need to hold your horses."

Taking Loki's advice literally, Mason reached up in alarm and grabbed the horse on his necklace in one fist. "Oh, good, you're still there," he murmured in relief.

"If my sister gave you the sun and moon, Yggdrasil would die," Frey yelled from across the room. "The World Tree needs both day and night to grow and, you know, stay alive."

"Exactly! Besides, I don't own the sun and the moon," Freya added to Mason. "So I couldn't give them to you anyway."

Loki had stopped laughing. His forehead was wrinkled now, as if he was thinking. "Hmm. Could you rebuild the wall in three days? Without help from anyone else?" he challenged the boy loudly enough for everyone in the Valhallateria to hear. Smiling at Freya, he said, "If Mason can do that, you'd agree to his terms, right? The sun, the moon, your heart?"

"What? No!" Freya scowled at Loki.

In a voice too low for Mason to hear, Loki coaxed her. "Look at him. He's scrawny. There's no way he can rebuild the wall that fast alone. But if he gets any work done in three days, it'll be a start. C'mon, just say yes."

He had a point, Freya thought. Others around them who'd been close enough to hear Loki's idea were nodding their heads in agreement. Only Angerboda, who was standing by the fountain, was glaring at her. Of course, that girl was crushing on Loki, which probably had something to do with her dislike of Freya. Did the girlgiant really imagine that Freya was crushing on him too? She most definitely was not!

Loki was cute and funny, she supposed, but everything was a joke to him. Plus, he was very stuck on himself and not exactly nice to others. She could think of another boy who was way more interesting. Freya's gaze found Od in the crowd. She liked that he was kind, acted serious, and didn't seem to know how cute he was.

Sure, he was a bit on the quiet side, but she liked that he didn't try to show off. Just then his gaze caught hers, and he quickly looked away. He was adorably shy, too!

Loki gestured toward Mason up on the table, then looked back at Freya. "Well?" he prodded.

"I'm thinking," Freya replied. She couldn't help it if her thoughts kept straying from the question at hand. This wasn't a decision she wanted to make!

With many hopeful eyes on her, she agonized over her response. Getting started on a new wall that was needed to protect Asgard, the school, and Yggdrasil was a good idea. And surely there was no chance of Mason finishing it in so short a time. If she was a good sport about this, maybe she could gain the goodwill of other students and reverse the bad impression she'd made so far.

Freya sighed. "Okay. I agree to the deal."

"Yes!" Mason shouted, hopping up and down in a happy circle atop her table. "I will build the wall in three days!" he crowed for all to hear. "When I succeed, I have been promised the sun and the moon. And Freya's heart, too!"

Freya hunched her shoulders, embarrassed. She was already regretting her decision. How had she let Loki and peer pressure talk her into it?

As if he'd guessed what she was thinking, Loki whispered to her, "Don't worry. He won't get it done."

Freya nodded curtly, wondering if she should have trusted her earlier instinct *not* to trust him. "You'd better hope not!" she whispered back fiercely.

"Off the table—immediately!" a bossy Valhallateria lady shouted at Mason. When the boy jumped down, a crowd gathered around to pepper him with questions about how he planned to accomplish his task.

The entire room was now abuzz. Freya hoped people didn't think she was really in like with Mason. If so, they were wrong, wrong, wrong!

"Are you really okay with this?" Frey asked, having come over.

When she shrugged uncertainly, Loki frowned. "I hope you won't break your promise. If you do, you'll hurt Mason's feelings big-time. And probably gain some enemies around here. Odin won't like it if he hears his new students aren't getting along."

"The Vanir don't break promises," Freya assured him.

"Good!" said Loki. Seeing that Mason was looking toward them, he shot the boy a cheery grin and a thumbs-up, as if to say that everything was going as planned.

"Awesome! Guess I'd better go get to work!" Mason called out happily. He sent Freya a thrilled smile. Then, even though it was already dusk, he hurried off to begin repairing the wall.

Freya took a step in his direction to stop him but then halted. She didn't want to hurt Mason's feelings or make everyone here at school think she was a liar by backing out. But, oh, how she did want to back out! Promise or not. In her role as the girlgoddess of love, she took the giving of hearts very seriously. She had never crushed on a boy and did not intend to crush on Mason. But what if he somehow succeeded in building the wall in three days? Fingers crossed on both hands that he wouldn't!

"Well, see you," Loki told her, ambling off. Probably afraid that if he stuck around, she would start yelling at him. Which she might have done if she'd thought it would help this situation!

"Hey, it's okay," Frey said to her after Loki was gone. "Nobody could build that wall in three days. Mason does look kind of skinny and weak. Not like me." Grinning, he posed for her, making a muscle with his arm. It wasn't a very big one, however.

She was in the middle of grinning back when, from the corner of her eye, she thought she caught a movement within the large painted friezes that covered the walls. Then something so weird happened that she jerked in surprise, momentarily forgetting her troubles.

"Frey! Look at that frieze," she hissed, pointing to a

scene of heroic warriors marching through a grove of fruit trees. "Did one of those warriors in it just move?"

Frey followed her gaze and gasped. "Yeah! And that one did too! And that one, see?"

At first it was only the blinking of eyes or the twitch of a hand, as if those carved, painted heroes were waking up from a long sleep. But soon they were all moving around within their friezes—stretching, walking, and even running!

"What's happening?" Freya wondered aloud. Nervous murmurs swept the Valhallateria as other students noticed what was going on too.

Suddenly every figure within the sculpted carvings seemed to come alive. And because they were all warriors, they immediately went into battle mode. Painted hands grabbed turnips, carrots, and crab apples from painted fields and trees or from platters on carved feast tables, depending on the scene. Arms drew back. Fists punched forth from the friezes. With resounding battle

cries, warriors hurled food across the room at warriors on opposite walls!

"Food fight!" someone yelled.

Heads, arms, and legs extended from the painted carvings as far as they could without the warriors themselves actually leaving them. The moment food was lobbed out of a frieze, it temporarily turned real. A dozen turnips from one frieze arced high overhead and entered another frieze on the other side of the Valhallateria, whacking the warriors carved within. *Thwack!* The attacked warriors pelted back deviled auk eggs and wild plums. *Splat! Thump!*

Meanwhile, the Valkyries had sprung into action from their watchful positions near the friezes. They rushed here and there, shooing students out in an orderly manner, as if they'd known this was going to happen.

"Hurry! Off to your dorms! Girls go to the right for Vingolf Hall. Boys turn left for Breidablik Hall! Find a pod within your hall and get settled in for the night. Sleep well! Classes begin tomorrow!"

Leaving behind whatever food remained on their plates, students bolted from the Valhallateria, giggling and dodging flying food. As Freya raced for the door, her boot heel struck a plum. "Whoa!" She slipped and fell to her knees, then scooted under a table to avoid being trampled by students streaming around her.

When the coast was temporarily clear, she leaped out. *Thonk!* A bread roll struck her shoulder and she grabbed it. Laughing, she took a bite of it to kill off the last of her hunger as she dashed out the exit.

Outside she shivered in the cold air. It was dark now, and a light snow was swirling. Too bad she didn't have her cloak; it was in her backpack, which Heimdall had sent ahead to the girls' dorm. She looked left, then right. She'd already forgotten which way to go.

Luckily, Od happened by. "Vingolf dorm is that way!" he told her, motioning with his arm. Flashing her a smile, he ran the other way. She followed his directions but somehow wound up standing before a building with a sign that read BREIDABLIK. Hey, wasn't that the name of the boys' dorm? Had Od tricked her? Was he going to turn out to be like Loki? She hoped not!

She got directions from another boy, who pointed her in the opposite direction—to the other side of the Valhallateria. No other girls were still outdoors when she finally saw the sign that read VINGOLF. Which meant she was the last to straggle inside the girls' dorm.

11
Podmates

FREYA SAW A NOTE HANGING ON A NOTICEBOARD in the mudroom beyond the front door to Vingolf Hall. It read:

> *Welcome to your dorm at Asgard Academy, girls!*
> *—Odin and Ms. Frigg, principals*

Racks full of wet boots and skis from other girls lined the mudroom walls. Freya slipped off her red-and-white-plaid snow boots and set them on one of the racks. Then she pushed through another set of doors and padded into the main hall in her wool socks. As she came to a halt, her mouth fell open in awe.

Vingolf was as big as the outdoor village square back home! Only, the dorm was round, not square, and enclosed with a roof. A hole at the top vented smoke from the fire that burned in a pit at the room's center. Game tables, reading nooks, and gathering spaces were positioned all around the roaring fire.

She moved farther inside, bypassing a bunch of stools and small tables set with oil lamps carved from soapstone. Light for students to do homework by, she supposed.

Where did everyone sleep, though? Maybe through the doors all along the wall? She counted eighteen of them. She peered through the first open door she found and saw it did indeed lead into a bedroom with six hammocks for beds. There were six light-elves inside, all giggling and twirling, having so much fun that they didn't notice her.

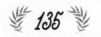

Like petals growing outward from the center pistil of a flower, the eighteen rooms were evenly spaced all around the edge of the circular main space of Vingolf. The next room she passed was occupied by girl dwarfs. Catching sight of Freya, a silver-eyed one sent her a hesitant smile, probably thinking that Freya wanted to room with them. "Sorry, no space," the girl called out, shrugging in an apologetic way. "There are five of us and only five podbeds."

"Okay, thanks," said Freya. So the hammocks were called podbeds? Interesting. She returned the dwarf girl's small smile with a big, friendly one that made all five dwarfs blink. She was still hoping to make a good impression on behalf of her world and didn't want anyone around here to think the Vanir were standoffish or unfriendly, in spite of what Angerboda had hinted at back on the Bifrost Bridge.

Freya moved on. The other open rooms she passed were of various sizes, some smaller and others larger, with podbeds for four to eight girls. Each room also had a small window on its far wall and a large rug woven with the big initials *AA*, for "Asgard Academy." The central fire was making the dorm rather warm, so many of the windows' shutters were partly open to let in some air.

So far the rooms she'd passed were already filled with girls putting away their stuff and chatting. Some looked at her curiously, but none invited her in. Like Njord had noted on their trip here, students from the same world were sticking together. Even in these podrooms, it seemed.

To her relief, Freya eventually spotted her backpack on the floor outside one of the podroom doors. She hurried toward it. Did finding it here mean she'd been assigned to this particular pod? When she straightened from picking up her pack, she saw that there were already some girls in the room. Angerboda and five other girlgiants. *Oh no!*

"Want something?" demanded Angerboda, seeing her standing there.

"Um . . ." Freya poked her head through the doorway and glanced around. There was one empty bed.

Angerboda followed the direction of her gaze. "We're full," she said quickly.

Freya frowned. It was not like she *wanted* to room with this mean girlgiant! Still, she *did* need a place to sleep. A wave of homesickness washed over her, and she wished she were back in her village in Vanaheim in her own cozy home with her own comfy bed. Back there she'd had many friends and everyone had welcomed her!

"Hey!" said a familiar, friendly voice behind her. It was Skade. She took Freya's enormous bag from her, slinging it over one shoulder like it weighed nothing. Half-giants were strong! "C'mon. Want to room with us?" Skade asked.

"Us?" echoed Freya. Two more girlgiants, she assumed Skade meant.

Skade nodded absently but didn't elaborate as she headed off. Uncertainly Freya followed her across the hall and past the fire pit to another of the bedrooms.

"Don't worry about Angerboda," Skade advised. "She's always on some kind of rampage. In Jotunheim her kenning is 'distress-bringer.'"

"Well deserved," mumbled Freya, which made Skade laugh.

The two girls already inside Skade's dorm room looked up when Freya and Skade entered. One of them was Idun, the apple juice girl from the Valhallateria. The other was a stranger.

Upon seeing Freya, the unknown girl smiled curiously and twisted a strand of her long hair around one finger. It was stunningly beautiful—the golden color of wheat in sunlight. "Come on in," she told Freya, waving her inside. "I'm Sif. That's Idun."

"Yeah, we've met," said Freya. She smiled at Idun,

who paused to smile back while in the act of hanging a white linen shift in a small closet.

"We have one hammock—I mean, podbed—left," said Sif.

Freya eyed the one empty hammock uncertainly. There was already stuff on the floor alongside it. A pair of skis and ski poles, and a pair of ski boots, too. Her heart sank a little. Had it already been claimed by another girl who wasn't here yet?

She nodded toward the empty hammock. "That one? But there's someone else's stuff—"

"Oops, that's my junk. Sorry," said Skade, running over to gather up the ski stuff. Then she set Freya's pack on the hammock, sending it swinging.

Still Freya hesitated. They all seemed friendly, but if she roomed here, she would be the only girl from Vanaheim in a pod of three Asgard girls. On the other hand, if they were willing to give her a chance, she'd give them one back!

"So did you all know each other before coming here?" she asked the others as she opened the small closet that stood beside her bed.

Idun shook her head, causing her long light-brown hair to sway. "Nuh-uh. Asgard is a big place. None of us had ever met before, even though we're all Aesir."

Learning that the other three girls were also new to one another made Freya feel a little better. Relaxing some, she said, "Vanaheim is big too, with lots of villages. I haven't met everyone there, either, not by a long shot."

Freya turned to her hammock. *"Hó!"* she exclaimed. It was an expression of surprise she'd learned from Gullveig that basically meant "whoa!" "Is this thing a *real seedpod*?"

"Mm-hmm, all the hammocks are. Minus the seeds," said Skade.

"We think they must have come from the World Tree, judging by how humongous they are," said Sif.

Freya nodded, eyeing her hammock's nearly six-foot length. Ropes tied at either end of it were attached to sturdy hooks in the ceiling. The minute she touched her pack, the seedpod bed went swinging again. "This hammock thingy is going to take some getting used to." She moved her pack onto the floor beneath it for now.

As she straightened again, a large black bird holding something that looked like a baby-size red wool sock in its beak came flapping in through the room's only window. Its arrival startled Sif into dropping the fistfuls of ribbons and other hair accessories she'd just pulled from her bag. Some fell onto her podbed, and the rest tumbled to the wood-plank floor.

Opening its black beak, the bird plunked the red wool sock thing onto Freya's podbed. Then it cawed and flew back out.

"What in the nine worlds?" Idun exclaimed in surprise.

Skade dropped the pair of boots she'd been holding

and raced to the window to watch the bird flap away. "It's one of Odin's ravens!" She closed the shutters against the cold air and turned excitedly toward Freya. "What did it bring you?"

"Not sure exactly." Freya held up the lopsided red thing. It looked like the knitting project Ms. Frigg had begun when they met in the throne room with Odin earlier. A note attached to the red object confirmed her guess. It read:

> *To replace the pouch you lost.*
> *—Ms. Frigg*

Gulp! Somehow Ms. Frigg knew she'd lost a pouch on the bridge. Did she know what it had contained? Did that mean Odin knew too? *Hope not!* thought Freya.

"So what do you think it is?" Sif asked as she gathered up her hair decorations and stuck them on the high shelf in her small closet.

Freya waved the note. "It's supposed to be a pouch," she informed the girls.

"From Ms. Frigg?" asked Idun and Skade at the same time.

"How'd you guess?" asked Freya.

"It wasn't hard," Skade said, sharing a look of amusement with Sif and Idun.

"Ms. Frigg is kind of famous in Asgard for her knitting gifts," Idun explained quickly. "The yarn she spins is beautiful and strong."

"But when she knits you something, it's usually . . . *unusual*," added Sif.

"She's the kind of person who would accidentally knit you a holiday sweater with one arm longer than the other, or maybe a lopsided hat," said Skade.

Smiling, Freya held up her gift. "Or a lumpy, pointy-ended pouch? It was nice of her, though. Especially since we only just met."

"Really? You've met Ms. Frigg already?" Idun said.

"Oh, wait. You're the girlgoddess that Odin called to their office, right?" Having finished hanging up various items of clothing in the small closet next to her pod-bed, she stowed her empty bag below her hammock.

Freya tied the pouch onto one of her necklaces. "Yeah, I guess that's how I'll be known from now on: the girlgoddess that Odin called to the office on her very first day at the academy."

The other girls laughed, but she sensed their curiosity about her trip to see the two principals, so she explained. "He wanted to ask about the kind of magic I do. I imagine he'll be asking all students the same question sooner or later. The ones who have magic, anyway. I just happened to go first."

Skade cocked her head at Freya. "So what kind of magic *can* you do?"

"I can see," Freya replied casually.

"Huh?" asked Idun.

"I'm a seer," Freya explained. "I can see the future."

145

It wasn't really a lie. Although she couldn't see the future right now, she definitely hoped to change that very soon by getting Brising back from those jewel-snatching dwarfs down in Darkalfheim!

"Awesome," said Sif, studying her with new interest. "What else did Odin say?"

"He recited a poem or two that he made up on the spot. Nothing much else." When she kneeled to open her tightly stuffed bag, it practically exploded with clothes. She began stowing them away in her closet.

"So how about you guys? What are your magic skills?" asked Freya, hoping to change the subject.

"This." To everyone's amazement, Sif transformed herself into a rowan tree. Then she went from that to a swan. Then back to girlgoddess shape.

"Awesome!" said Freya, clapping her hands. "Wish I could shape-shift. What does it feel like when it happens? While you're transformed, can you understand what other trees or swans are thinking or feeling?"

Sif looked pleased at her interest. "Sort of. One time, when I was a swan, I was skimming over a lake and saw some tadpoles. They looked so delicious to my swan self that I almost ate one."

"Eew!" chorused the other three girls, giggling.

"My 'magic' is skiing. I'm an ace at it," Skade explained. "Also, I can grow bigger in a snap, which can come in handy, or be a problem if you're in a little space." Everyone giggled again. Then Freya, Sif, and Skade all looked at Idun.

"I just make juice, which you already know," said Idun in her soft, sweet voice. "I'm pretty sure that's why Odin invited me here to AA. Because I agreed to bring an *eski* full of the golden apples that grow in my grove to the Valkyries at the Valhallateria every day."

"*Eski?*" Skade echoed.

To explain, Idun pulled a tiny wooden box the size of a single ice cube from the pocket of her *hangerock*. "Behold my *eski*." When she gave the box a shake and set

147

it on the ground, it expanded into a box large enough to hold many apples. After this demonstration she folded her *eski* back to ice-cube size and pocketed it again.

As Skade and Sif asked Idun more about her special apples and *eski*, Freya pondered the closet she'd been given. Her clothes weren't going to fit. Her podmates didn't have the same problem, she noticed as she glanced around the room. Idun's and Sif's clothes neatly filled their closets without being squashed together. Skade's clothes filled her closet only two-thirds full!

Skade picked up her skis and boots and headed out their pod's door. "I'm going to stow these on the rack in the mudroom. Be right back."

"'Kay," Sif and Idun murmured.

Freya peered at the outside of her closet. It had hooks on each of its tall sides. *Phew!* She got busy hanging bulky outerwear things like her cloak and sweaters on the hooks, and sticking her other clothes *inside* the closet.

After a few minutes she noticed Idun and Sif staring

at her in stunned amazement. Or rather at her *clothes*. Did they think she had too many?

But then Idun gushed, "Your clothes are adorable!"

Sif nodded. "*Love* that teal *hangerock*."

Freya beamed. "Thanks. I designed and sewed everything myself. I'm kind of into fashion."

"Wow!" the two girls said, oohing and aahing over various items she unpacked.

The minute Freya finished emptying her bag, Skade rushed back in. "All the other girls are choosing pod names!" she informed them breathlessly.

Freya and her roomies stepped outside their pod. *Bam! Bam!* Various pod groups were using the heels of their snow boots as hammers to hang cute signs on their pod doors, naming their groups.

"Look, those light-elves are calling themselves the Shooting Stars," noted Sif. "And that other pod of light-elves is the Northern Lights."

"Angerboda's pod came up with the name Polar

Bears. One of the human pods is named Snowbells," said Skade.

"Awww! Those names are all so cute!" said Idun.

"Quick! We need a pod name too!" said Freya. It needed to be a good one. No way did she want to give those girlgiants an edge over her own group that could later get them teased.

They all quickly agreed they needed a name, but no one was sure what name to choose. For long moments they stood outside their pod, studying the signs of other groups and thinking hard.

"How about the Apple Turnovers?" Idun suggested at last. It was a name that suited her, of course, but not necessarily the rest of their group.

"Snow*cats*?" Freya suggested.

"Snow*swans*?" countered Sif.

"*Ski* Skunks?" said Skade. "Oh, wait, that name stinks."

The girls burst into giggles. The pod names they came up with afterward became sillier and sillier.

"Girl*pod*desses?"

"The Quad Pod?"

"The Podettes?"

"Think *Pod*sitive?"

They weren't coming up with usable names, but at least they were having fun! Freya felt happy. She was beginning to feel like part of a group, just like back home.

And then Angerboda had to ruin everything. She hefted a large mailbag, ambled over with two girlgiants from her pod, and dropped the bag at Freya's feet. "This came to our pod for you before you got here," Angerboda announced. "Forgot to mention it."

Humph! Since this bag of mail had apparently been delivered to the girlgiants' door, Freya guessed that whoever had brought her stuff to the dorm had intended her to share their pod all along. That was okay, though; she was glad she wasn't rooming with Angerboda.

As her podmates and the girlgiants looked on, Freya kneeled and opened the mailbag. As she'd expected, it was filled with slabs of wood, stone, metal, and bone. Angular symbols had been carved or burned into the slabs to form rune messages. Freya was accustomed to getting fan mail like this.

That nosy Angerboda leaned over and quickly read the runes on the topmost stone slab. "'Dear Freya: You are sooo beautiful. Will you be my girlfriend? Write back soon.'" The rune writer had glued a flower onto the stone too, but by now it had withered. It was time-consuming to write in runes, so the letters Freya got were usually short like that.

Freya closed the bag, but it was too late. Angerboda had read the letter aloud in such a booming voice that most of the girls in the dorm had probably heard it.

"How many boyfriends do you have, anyway?" Angerboda asked, eyeing the mailbag and wrinkling her nose.

Freya's gaze swept the circular hall, taking in the looks she was getting from girls who'd overheard. Many were simply curious or amused, but others appeared jealous or disapproving. Though Freya had never been in like with a boy, Angerboda was making it seem like all she cared about was boys! It wasn't her fault that tons of them wrote to say they were crushing on her. Most of them didn't even *know* her!

"None. No boyfriends," Freya replied loudly, hoping all these other girls would hear and believe her. "I'm the girlgoddess of love and beauty, so people write to me about their romantic problems. Sometimes with misguided crushes, too." Yes, Freya liked fashion and helping people with their in-like issues, but there was a lot more to her than Angerboda seemed to assume. It wasn't fair that this girl was trying to cut her down in front of her new podmates.

Angerboda sniffed snarkily. "Mm-hmm. Sure." Having drawn negative attention to Freya, the snooty girlgiant smiled smugly. Then she and her friends turned on their heels and left.

Luckily, a banging sound shifted everyone's attention to the main hall doors. "Look! Class schedules are being posted!" a cheery light-elf called out. She was bouncing on her toes and clapping her hands with excitement as some thin slabs of wood were tacked up on the inner doors by a Valkyrie holding a huge hammer. After she left, everyone gathered around to view the list.

Freya didn't really want to look. It had never been her plan to stick around AA long enough to get involved in classes. She probably shouldn't have even unpacked her bag! Still, she supposed it was too much to hope that she'd rescue Brising, find Gullveig, and talk Frey into returning to Vanaheim before first period tomorrow, so she might as well check for her name. As it turned out, the list only showed which class each student would report to first. In her case, it was Norse History.

Later, before she went to bed, she opened the shutters and looked out her pod's small window. Gazing up into the leafy branches of the splendid World Tree, she suddenly wondered, *Where are the classrooms?*

Then, deciding that question would have to go unanswered till morning, Freya closed the shutters again and snuggled under her covers in her podbed. Because, *brr*, it was cold outside!

12
Cool Classes

THE GIRLS LEFT VINGOLF HALL THE NEXT
morning at the same time that the boys poured out
of Breidablik. For the first day of classes (maybe her
only day of classes, if she could quickly accomplish her
secret to-do list!), Freya was wearing another favorite outfit. This one was a woolly gray *hangerock* with
embroidered red felt leaves, overhung with her nine
necklaces.

Since the Valhallateria stood between the two dorm

halls, the students all wound up going inside to breakfast together. Everything felt rushed and confused on this first morning of school. Freya didn't even get to speak to Frey till they met on their way outside again after eating.

"Happy Frey-day!" she told him. Because this day of the week, Friday, had been named in his honor when he was born.

He grinned at her. "Thanks." They were standing alone. Now was her chance to start him thinking about the idea of returning home. However, just as she was about to launch into that topic, Kvasir and Njord came along, and then Frey's new friends Thor, Bragi, Od, and Loki joined them too.

"I wonder where the classrooms are?" Thor said as more and more kids gathered, standing around and also wondering where to go.

And then something happened that made Freya forget for the time being about bringing up her back-to-Vanaheim plan. Out of nowhere doors suddenly appeared to hover in midair, scattered high and low among Yggdrasil's leafy branches with no visible means of support. *Pop! Pop! Pop!* Signs sprang up along the golden forest fernway to indicate which doors opened to which classes.

The doors took intriguing shapes, not just the usual rectangles, but circles and triangles and trapezoids, and even object and animal shapes as well. Seeing Freya, Idun came over and asked, "What do you think is holding them up?"

"Magic, I imagine," answered Skade. Along with Sif, she had come up behind Freya, Idun, and the boys.

"Look! Aren't those little baby Bifrost bridges cute?" Sif added.

Freya had been so busy studying the doors that she hadn't noticed the numerous small tricolor rainbow bridges that had also popped up here and there, high among Yggdrasil's leaves. A series of branch ladders, vine tunnels, vine swings, and vine slides had also materialized. In combination, these would allow students to travel up, down, and around the branches to get wherever they needed to go.

Showing no caution at all, Skade grabbed a fragile-looking vine swing that hung from a branch overhead, sat on its seat, and began swinging. "Wheee! I'm off to Dragon-Dodging class!" she yelled excitedly. When she'd swung high enough, she leaped off the swing onto a wide branch and then disappeared through a dragon-shaped door.

"Right behind you!" called Thor, following her.

"Ditto!" said Bragi, Kvasir, and Njord, who were also in that class.

Seconds later Idun and Sif waved bye as they scrambled up branch ladders to their first-period class together. Its door was round, and a sign on the path indicated that the class was called Odin's Eye.

"Hope I get that class later," Od remarked. He had come up beside Freya without her noticing.

"Me too!" enthused Freya. It sounded fascinating. Of course, she wouldn't be around to take that class or any other for long, since she planned to return to Vanaheim.

Freya, Frey, Loki, and Od walked along a branch-way with other students, searching for signs that would point them toward their first-period classrooms. As they walked, the sounds of construction reached their ears from somewhere far below. *Bam! Crunch!*

Frey sent Freya a sideways look. "Sounds like Mason is hard at work on the wall."

"Not too hard, I hope," Freya said earnestly. With everything that had happened since dinner, she'd temporarily managed to put Mason out of her mind. But now she stood on tiptoe and craned her neck. Unfortunately, Yggdrasil's branches grew too thick along the path for her to see down to the wall.

"Don't worry," Loki assured her. "That wall would

take three *seasons* for anyone working alone to rebuild. He has only three *days*."

Having stopped at a sign that read TREE LORE, Frey sat on the edge of a vine slide. "This one's mine. See you at the V for lunch if I don't see you before!" he exclaimed to the others. Then he launched himself into the slide and looped the loop upward toward a door shaped like one of Yggdrasil's giant ash-tree leaves.

"The V?" Freya repeated, scrunching her nose in confusion.

"Short for 'Valhallateria,'" explained Od. "I heard some other kids calling it that too. Probably came up with the nickname because of the V-shaped door handles."

Freya nodded as they continued on along the path. "Good. Because 'Val-whatchamacalla-teria' is really a mouthful!"

Od laughed, then sent her a more serious look. "Hey,

um, sorry about last night. I had the two dorms mixed up. Didn't mean to send you to the boys' one. I wound up at Vingolf, which was kind of embarrassing. Made a couple of girls scream when I stuck my head inside the main room."

Freya laughed. "Poor you. But s'okay. Unlike you, I realized the mistake before I went in the wrong door." She was glad he hadn't tricked her, because that meant her estimation of his good character hadn't been mistaken.

"Od wound up lost in the snow for, like, an hour last night," Loki teased. "He was practically a snowsicle by the time he finally found his way to Breidablik. Despite the fact that the two halls aren't far apart."

"Oh no!" Freya said, gazing at the other boy in concern.

Od shrugged. Good-naturedly he said, "What can I say? I have no sense of direction, so I get lost easily." Still, he seemed a little embarrassed by Loki's remark.

Freya tactfully changed the subject. Looking around, she said to Od, "I wonder which way Norse History is?"

"You're brave to ask me about directions after last night," he replied, chuckling. "But I think that could be it." He pointed to a sign at her feet that read NORSE HISTORY.

She giggled at having missed seeing it. Then she looked straight up above the sign to see a door shaped like a ship.

"I have history first too," Loki told her.

"And that's my class," said Od, pointing at another sign. With a smile and a nod at Freya and Loki, he headed up a branch ladder on the opposite side of the path to a class called Gnashing and Smashing.

"See you," Freya called after him. Then she and Loki started over the mini Bifrost bridge that connected to their classroom. Instead of going through the ship-shaped class door right away, though, Freya ducked her head around it first to confirm that, just like that blue office door yesterday, there was nothing behind this door either.

Loki grinned. "These doors are pretty strange, aren't they?" he said. Then he pushed through the ship door, which immediately opened into a classroom that looked like the inside of a big wooden sailing ship! "Cool! They're actually some kind of weird portals!"

Freya entered behind him. "I guess they each lead to a different classroom?"

"Hall," corrected a sleepy-sounding grown-up voice. "Here at Asgard Academy we call them halls, not classrooms."

The voice belonged to their teacher, Snorri Sturluson. So named, they soon discovered, because during class he tended to fall asleep and *snore* very easily! But his class was still super interesting and went by in a flash. Toward the end of it he supplied each student with a verbal list of the rest of their classes. It wasn't practical to write everything down when it meant carving into wood or stone, so students had to memorize their lists as the teacher recited them. Freya repeated her other four classes over and over to herself: Odin's Eye (yay!), Runes, Findings, and Ragnarok Survival Skills.

After Heimdall tooted his horn to signal the end of first period, students emptied out of their hall doors. They were eager to find friends and compare schedules to see if they shared the same classes.

Freya was crossing another of the baby Bifrost bridges when she heard loud thumping and smashing that sounded like huge rocks clashing together. Mason must *really* be working hard, she thought uncomfortably. He was out of view at the moment, but from her vantage point she could see the wall now. Already, gaps in it had been filled in, and it was much taller than before. He was making surprising progress. She bit her lip. What if he succeeded?

Freya jumped when someone behind her made

a kissing sound. *Mwah!* She whipped around to see Angerboda with two of her girlgiant pals. They must have noted the headway Mason was making on the wall too. Angerboda had made the kissy noise to tease her about that promise to give her heart to Mason if he finished his task.

"Gosh! Was that a sneeze? I hope you aren't catching a cold," Freya replied politely, pretending she'd misunderstood.

Angerboda frowned but then perked up again. "I'm fine. But I've got a *giant* feeling you'll be facing a *wall* of disappointment soon."

Her friends giggled at that, but Freya didn't find it at all funny!

"Freya! Come look!" It was Frey. He beckoned her over to another baby Bifrost bridge a short distance away where he and Loki stood looking downward. Here they could easily see both the wall and Mason through Yggdrasil's branches.

Freya gasped. Mason was no longer scrawny! He had muscles now and stood ten feet tall! If that wasn't enough bad news, he'd found an enormous, strong-looking white-spotted brown horse to help him move the stones. "Mason's a giant? But he has those bushy eyebrows. I thought he was human!"

"I guess some giants have bushy eyebrows too," said Frey. "Besides, I just noticed his eyebrows have a lot of white in them. Must be a frost giant."

Just then Mason looked up and spotted the three of them on the bridge. Immediately he shrank to nongiant size. Cupping his hands around his mouth, he shouted up to her and waved. "Hi, Freya!"

"Cheater!" Loki yelled down at him. "You said the wall would keep us safe from Jotunheim. But if you're a frost giant, you're *from* Jotunheim!"

"Never said I wasn't," said Mason. "And you didn't ask. Plus, I only said the wall would protect against *troublemakers*."

"You're *still* cheating, though. You can't use a helper!" shouted Frey. He pointed at the horse.

Mason folded his arms, looking stubborn. "Loki said I can't be helped by *anyone else*. A horse is not an *anyone*, because that refers to people." As the horse easily nudged another heavy stone into place in the wall, he gave it a fond pat and told it, "Good boy, Unlucky."

"Unlucky. That's the name of that carved horse he wore on a cord around his neck! It must be magical," Loki said.

Just like my tabby cats! thought Freya. "Oh, great," she moaned. In her opinion, that helpful horse really was unlucky. For her!

Tooot! Heimdall's horn sounded just then, so they all had to take off for second period. In her Odin's Eye class things started looking up. And down and all around. The focus of the class, she learned, would be on using a huge, super-magnifying telescope called the

Eye that could flex and sneakily extend to let them gaze almost anywhere! She had wondered how Odin could keep track of all the worlds at once. Now she knew. She felt a pang of disappointment that she didn't plan to be here long enough to get really good at using this amazing telescope!

In third-period Runes class they spent time outdoors using wooden wands to draw runes in the snow. The teacher said that later, after they'd reviewed more symbols, they'd learn to foretell destiny with the use of small, carved rune stones. She would have liked to keep taking this class as well.

Then came lunch, which she shared with her three podmates. While eating, they continued to come up with possible names for their pod in Vingolf.

"Yggdragirls?"

"The Pod Squad?"

Idun sighed. "Those don't feel quite right."

Freya nodded. "Let's face it—they're just not *us*."

"Yeah, we need something with girl power," said Skade.

"The Norse Force?" suggested Sif.

Although they kind of liked this one, they were still unsure about it, so they kept tossing around ideas. All the while Freya couldn't help imagining what might be going on back home at her old school. Her Vanaheim friends would be making jewelry without her and practicing ice-skating drills without her. Were they missing her? She missed doing all the familiar, fun things they'd done together. Despite the interesting classes and these nice podmate girls, being here at AA was a tough change!

After lunch she had two more classes to go. The hall for her fourth-period Findings class was at the top of a branch ladder. Its portal door was made of real, dazzling gold studded with gemstones! As she gazed at the door in wonder, Ms. Frigg came by.

"Are you the Findings teacher?" Freya asked her in surprise.

Ms. Frigg shook her head and gestured toward another portal nearby. "I teach one class only—Runes, fourth period. My coprincipal duties keep me too busy for more."

"Oh. Well, I want to thank you for the pouch," Freya said sincerely. She held it out, showing Ms. Frigg that she'd strung it on one of her bead necklaces. "How did you know I'd lost one? Are you a seer too?" Freya asked, hoping this was not the case. She wasn't ready for Odin to find out the truth about Brising being gone!

Ms. Frigg laughed. "Goodness, no! Knitting and spinning are my talents. However, I suppose I can see in a way. I can tell when people are missing something, so I knit a replacement for them if I can."

If only Ms. Frigg could knit a mini version of the entire village of Vanaheim so Freya could carry it around with her always! The notion of a teeny, lopsided

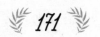

knitted replica of her village made her grin.

After Ms. Frigg had continued on to teach Runes, Freya pushed through the golden door to Findings. To her delight, it turned out to be a jewelry-making class with all the gold she could ever want for creating her designs. *Woo-hoo!* "Findings," she learned, was the general term for the tools they would use to make their jewelry.

Her last class of the day was Ragnarok Survival Skills. Its door was dark wood that was divided into nine rectangles, each carved with a scene to represent one of the nine worlds. Once through the portal, she entered a vast landscape with all kinds of climbing walls and obstacle courses. She quickly spotted Loki, Thor, Od, Skade, and Idun in the class. Idun motioned her over to sit with her on a large rock, and they both waved to Skade where she sat with some girlgiants. There were no chairs. Everyone else sat on the ground or on rocks too.

Suddenly Heimdall, the security guard, walked in.

"Welcome, Asguardians! And I'm spelling that with a *u* as in 'guard,'" he boomed. "Because learning to guard Asgard is what you'll be doing here."

Freya and Idun shared confused glances. Somehow they were going to learn how to *guard Asgard* Academy?

"I'll be your teacher this period. Every student at this school will spend one hour a week here at this guard post with me, acquiring skills that will keep Ragnarok at bay," Heimdall went on.

Huh? This classroom is a guard post? Freya recalled the word "Ragnarok" from that button on the column behind the goat fountain in the V. She had a feeling they would all soon be told what that button-under-glass was for, and that it would be something unpleasant.

"If he's teaching this class, who's watching the bridge?" she whispered to Idun.

"Good question," Idun whispered back.

Heimdall whipped around. "This *is* the bridge!" he informed them. "Or rather my hall, Himinbjorg, which overlooks it." He stood at least twenty feet away. How had he managed to hear them talking?

"Be aware that I can hear the grass grow! I can even hear the wool grow on sheep. And I hear when students whisper, too." Heimdall didn't name names, but Freya and Idun knew he meant them, and sent each other sheepish looks.

"Someday we will battle a terrible foe that will spill out from one of the worlds to attack us!" Heimdall continued, pacing back and forth among the students now. "There will be a long winter. A great fire. Mighty Yggdrasil will shudder and quake. A great serpent will be unleashed. The alarm button in the Valhallateria will sound five hundred and forty blasts! It will be us against monsters! Doomsday!"

Doomsday? Freya had heard that word too often recently—beginning with Brising's future-telling. Ragnarok must be the doomsday her jewel had meant! The one that could be stopped by the power of that mysterious secret world. And that "X540" on the button in the V? It must refer to the alarm's five hundred and forty blasts.

"Doomsday, huh. Well, that sounds . . . fun," joked Od, who broke the silence that had fallen and made everyone laugh.

He had said just the right thing to ease the tension. Her crush had a sense of humor, too! Freya sat up straighter on her rock perch. Wait a minute! *Crush?* Was she really crushing on a boy? Not exactly. Not yet, anyway. But for the first time she kind of cared whether or not a particular boy liked her. Her whole world had just been ragnarocked!

She smiled to herself at the word she'd just made up. It was perfect for describing a time when your own personal inside-yourself world was so totally shaken up that heads felt like tails and you went from feeling normal to feeling weird. Basically, like what had been happening to her for the last two days.

Snapping back to attention, Freya heard Heimdall assuring the class that with proper preparation and caution, the real Ragnarok could be avoided for a long, long time.

"I hope it never comes!" she blurted out. The end of the worlds was a scary thing to contemplate, so it was good they could do something to keep that day from coming too soon.

"Not me—I look forward to the fight!" shouted Thor. The boys all cheered.

Freya and many of the girls rolled their eyes.

"Girls are every bit as good at fighting, though. If we ever have to!" said Skade.

"Yeah!" shouted the girls.

When Heimdall dismissed them later, Idun went to chat with Skade. But Freya walked superfast out of the hall, not wanting to talk to anyone, especially Od, until she figured out her feelings. She hardly even knew that boy, so how could she know if she was really in like with him?

School was over, and none of the teachers had given her any homework yet. It seemed like the perfect time to sneak away and go snooping in Darkalfheim for her jewel. Freya was nearing the Bifrost Bridge when she noticed Heimdall already there, standing guard. He would probably ask her a bunch of nosy questions about where she was off to. Should she tell him the truth about her destination? It was said that dwarfs were unpredictable and that you could get lost forever in their underground tunnels, so he'd likely try to talk her out of going where she needed to go.

Her kittycart! Instead of crossing the bridge, she would use that to fly to Darkalfheim. She veered into the nearby golden forest, where no one would notice her take off in it.

Walking along the fernway, she could hear Mason working on the wall in the distance. *Bam!* went his sledge-hammer. *Snort!* went his horse. After learning about Ragnarok, she now realized how important rebuilding

the protective wall really was. So it was actually a good thing he was working on it.

Still, she didn't want to have to make good on her promise to give her heart to a boy who wasn't special to her. He couldn't finish in time, right? Just in case, before two more days could pass, she needed to find Brising and Gullveig, and also talk Frey into going home!

Bam! Bam! Snort! Snort!

Freya sped off, trying to escape the worrisome sounds.

13
Gullveig

IN THE GOLDEN WOODS FREYA SLOWED AS SHE
passed the spot where the little slot door had slid open
in Yggdrasil's tree trunk the previous day. She was the
only one in this forest right now. Since school was out,
other students were either on Ragnarok guard duty,
studying, playing games, or hanging out to wait for
dinner.

She paused and rapped her knuckles on the bark,

not really expecting anything to happen. "Hey, you in there! Knock, knock!"

Ka-chunk! To her shock, the bark slid open just like the first time! Eyes stared back at her from the slot in the tree. Not those brown ones. No, she'd recognize *these* eyes anywhere. This was Gullveig!

"Amma!" A rush of joy filled her. But what was Gullveig doing inside Yggdrasil's trunk? And why did she look strangely close, yet also far away?

"Freya! I'm so glad to see you," said Gullveig, her dear face creasing into wrinkles as she smiled. Atop her gray hair she wore a blue wool hat that Freya had embroidered for her with glittery white snowflakes.

"What are you doing in there?" Freya exclaimed.

Before her *amma* could reply, they heard voices from somewhere down the fernway that led to the Valhallateria. "Someone's coming," said Gullveig. "Quick. Use your fingertip to trace the words 'Knowledge is power' on your palm," she ordered. "Then step forward until your nose and toes press against the tree."

"What?" Feeling a little foolish, Freya did as instructed.

Whoosh! Instantly she found herself standing inside a hollowed-out space in the very middle of the tree trunk, with Gullveig beside her. It took powerful magic to transport something as big as an entire girl through tree bark all the way to the center of the World Tree— Yggdrasil magic!

She and Gullveig hugged joyfully, grinning at each other. Then Freya gazed about in wonder. They were standing on a round wooden floor about two hundred feet across with a large hole in its center, through which she could view numerous other floors below them with similar holes. Several transparent tubular slides that ranged from about one to four feet in diameter cork-screwed up through the holes from somewhere far below.

The tree's curved inner walls were lined with runebook-filled shelves that extended as far downward as the eye could see. There were ladders on wheels that followed tracks here and there along the shelves, so by climbing from one ladder to another, all the other floors and their books could be reached. Comfy seating areas were haphazardly placed throughout the space.

"What are you doing here? What is this place?" Freya asked.

"Got myself a job," the old sorceress replied proudly. "Been working here in the Heartwood Library for Mimir."

"Who's Mimir?" asked Freya, not seeing anyone else around. Suddenly a column of bright-blue water shot up through one of the tubular slides to bubble in a tall fountainlike spout at eye level. Atop the spout sat a . . . *head*!

"Someone call me?" asked the head. *Glub, glub.*

"Freya, this is Mimir, the *head* librarian," Gullveig said to her.

"Pleased to meet you," Freya told Mimir. She almost laughed at the idea of calling him the head librarian but managed to stop herself in time. She didn't want to hurt Mimir's feelings!

He bowed his head graciously. "Welcome to the Heartwood Library." Heartwood was a tree's hardest wood, located at its center, Freya knew, so this was a fitting name.

"Mimir's incredibly smart," Gullveig went on. "He's known in all nine worlds for the extent of his knowledge."

"I don't know everything," Mimir admitted. "But what I don't know, I can usually find in a book."

Wow! What she wouldn't give to have a brain like Mimir's. But only if it were in a head connected to a body!

There were so many questions Freya wanted to ask right now. Like: Why were Gullveig and Mimir in here? Who had originally built this library? Also, how could a head live without a body, anyway?

But then she noticed that Mimir's eyes were brown, and something clicked. "It was your eye that looked out at me from Yggdrasil's trunk yesterday! And you I saw in the heart vision I had at Gullveig's hut, too!" she exclaimed to Mimir.

He nodded, which caused him to gently bob atop the waterspout. "Correct. Gullveig told me I could trust you not to tell anyone our whereabouts, so I summoned you here."

Then Freya had another *aha* moment. The *Heart*wood Library? This place had to be the secret world Brising had been talking about in its prophecy two days ago:

> *Adventure for you is about to start.*
> *In Asgard you must find the heart.*
> *A secret world there hides away*
> *That holds the power to stop doomsday!*

But how could a library stop Ragnarok? she wondered. Then her eyes wandered to the sign at the front of the library:

THE HEARTWOOD LIBRARY
Knowledge Is Power

Of course! Libraries were totally full of knowledge. And somehow the stuff in this library was going to save them from doom. She'd figured out Brising's future-telling! There were a lot of books here, though. Which one had the necessary knowledge? Time would tell, she hoped.

Freya cocked her head at Mimir curiously. "Why did you say that stuff about Yggdrasil needing me?"

"Because it's true. Gullveig says you have gifts, magical ones. War is very hard on Yggdrasil. But with your abilities and mine, and perhaps the magic of others, too, we can help the World Tree survive all this fighting," explained Mimir.

His words confused Freya. First off, she had only one gift—future-seeing magic, which she needed her jewel to do. And secondly, what war was he talking about? The Asgard-Vanaheim war had ended, and Ragnarok had not begun (and hopefully never would!). Before she could ask, Gullveig spoke up again.

"I'm so happy you've come." Gullveig picked up a small branch from a pile of them on a table and began whittling it to a thinner shape. She had made wands back in Vanaheim, too, capable of magic that could do simple tasks. "All this hiding has grown tiresome. It'll be nice for Mimir and me to have company. You're such a joy to have around, always good at finding a bright side during dark times." Having finished a wand, she sent it off to dust a shelf on its own and began another.

"Dark times? Why are you hiding?" asked Freya, growing more confused by the minute.

"The *why* should be obvious," began Mimir. "The war."

"It's the *what* we're hiding that's the secret," Gullveig finished. Tossing her whittling aside, she marched over to a large, ancient-looking leather trunk in the shadows of the stairs and opened it. It was full of gold!

Alarmed, Freya exclaimed, "Then the rumors are true? You stole Asgard's gold?"

"What? No!" Gullveig let go of the trunk's lid and it bammed shut. "I'm helping Mimir *protect* it from thieves who might like to steal it while Asgard's defenses are down."

Phew! So Gullveig hadn't stolen gold because of Freya's wish to have some for jewelry making after all. Hooray!

"This all started when Odin sent Mimir on a diplomatic mission to Vanaheim," Gullveig explained.

"You were in Vanaheim?" Freya gazed at Mimir in surprise.

He nodded, causing his head to bob up and down on top of the waterspout. "Briefly. And while I was there, a slight misunderstanding caused me to lose my head, er, body."

Picking up the thread of the story, Gullveig sent him a fond smile. "Got in way over his *head* in a situation he couldn't make *heads* or tails of." She laughed merrily and Mimir joined in.

"Ha-ha!" he guffawed. "Stop! You're going to make me laugh my *head* off!" He spun around and around in a way that looked rather dangerous to Freya. She held her breath, fearing his head might fall to the floor and roll away! But *phew*! That didn't happen.

Abruptly, Mimir stopped spinning, his eyes going serious. "Odin once asked me to safeguard Asgard's gold if trouble ever started. So when Gullveig spotted some frost giants stealing it, we stole it back."

Gullveig nodded. "Saw 'em hide the gold in a fresh-water pool we call the Spring of Mimir near Jotunheim."

She gestured at the spout Mimir sat upon. "We discovered this tubular water slide runs through one of Yggdrasil's roots, from that spring all the way up here."

"And that's how we found this library," Mimir said with a huge smile. "Purely by accident. In fact, the books in here helped us reverse engineer this slide. *Whooshed* the gold out from under the frost giants' giant noses and all the way up here. Before we could get word to Odin, war broke out. Gullveig set her magic wands to organizing this place, and we sat tight."

"Feels like home now," Gullveig said proudly. "Not even Odin knows about this library, I'll bet. You'll be safe in here with us until this horrible war ends," she added, coming over to pat Freya's hand.

Wait! Thoughts were bubbling around in Freya's brain, connecting themselves. Did these two think the war between Asgard and Vanaheim had actually been a war between Asgard and the frost giants? And that that war was still going on? Could Odin have forgotten he'd

189

asked Mimir to safeguard the gold in case of trouble? Maybe those frost giants had seen Gullveig sneaking off with the gold and reported that she'd stolen it? Probably on purpose to make Asgard mad at Vanaheim! So maybe those giants had caused the war, not Gullveig.

Before Freya could discuss these guesses with her *amma* and the librarian, Mimir went a little cross-eyed and then began spinning again. He went faster and faster, twirling crazily in place atop the roiling water and spattering drops every which way.

"What's going on?" Freya asked, ducking the spray.

"He's getting an insight," Gullveig murmured in excitement. "Sort of an intelligent vision based on his collective knowledge and observation."

Seconds later Mimir stopped spinning as suddenly as he'd started. He stared hard at Freya. "You keep fiddling with that broken gold chain you wear. You lost something important, didn't you? Tell me where you hope to find it, and I'll help you get there."

190

Surprised, Freya blurted, "Darkalfheim."

Mimir raised his eyebrows and gave her the expected warning. "The dwarfs there are tricksters, and their tunnels are dangerous."

"But they took my jewel," explained Freya. "I have to get it back."

"They took Brising?" Gullveig echoed. With a disgusted huff, she went back to her wand making again, muttering about jewel thieves.

"Very well, then," Mimir told Freya, directing his eyes downward. "One of these water slides will take you where you need to go. It ends in the Spring of Mimir, on the second world ring between Jotunheim and Darkalfheim."

As his words died away, Gullveig's eyes lit with concern. "No, I don't think so. It's too dangerous. She's safer here with us." Jumping up, she waved her wand back and forth in a negative gesture to emphasize her words.

Unfortunately, this caused the magic in the wand to zap out toward Freya and give her a push. She lost her footing and fell backward onto one of the slides. Instantly she was *whooshed* downward through it!

"Wait! I need to tell you something," Freya called. "The war is *overrr!*" However, she knew she had already fallen too far away for them to hear that last bit.

Everything became a blur as she swooshed down, down, down. Along the way she caught glimpses of strange curiosities crammed between books shelved on the curved walls of the lower library. A sculpture of a grotesque monster. An endlessly spinning top. A carved wooden army of fanciful animals. The title of two extra-large, fancy books caught her eye: *The Poetic Edda* and *The Prose Edda*. The latter had the words BY SNORRI STURLUSON lettered below its title. Her sleepy Norse History teacher had written it!

Abruptly the slide came to an end, and Freya shot out of it. *Splash!* She landed sitting in a bubbling pool that nourished one of Yggdrasil's three great roots. Grabbing a clump of wildflowers, she pulled herself out of the Spring of Mimir. *Clomp! Clomp!* Dripping wet, she'd expected to freeze half to death in the snow. However, she became immediately dry once her red-and-white-plaid snow boots touched the bank. The waters of the spring must be enchanted!

In the distance she spied mountains. Were they in Jotunheim or Darkalfheim? She looked the other way and saw caves. Someone—the dwarfs, she guessed—had carved the words DARKALFHEIM: KEEP OUT! across the side of a craggy black peak.

Well, that answered her question about which way to go. Ignoring the warning, she headed straight for the caves, following a stream.

A salmon leaped from the water from time to time, keeping pace with her as she walked. It was almost as if it was keeping an eye on her. When she veered away from the stream, she didn't notice the salmon changing form and moving onto land as a boygod. One with dark hair and dark-blue eyes. Unaware that she was being followed, she continued on, passing a glacier, ducking under an overhanging cliff, and then plunging down into a large cave.

As she felt her way through the chilly cave's dark tunnels, she moved toward the sound of clanking, which grew louder as she got closer to her goal. Eventually she saw orange and yellow sparks flying, and came upon the arched entryway to a blacksmith shop. A sign above the entry read:

Ivaldi's Sons:

Superfine Blacksmithing

(Way Better Than the Other Guys!)

What other guys? she wondered as she stepped into the forge. Darkalfheim dwarfs were all known to be skilled metalworkers. Different groups of them must compete for work. Which group had Brising, though?

Immediately she spotted four dwarfs at work. *Clink!* *Clank!* went their hammers, flattening gold. There were portraits of them displayed on a far wall, with their names written in gold leaf: Alfrigg, Berling, Dvalin, Grerr.

When they moved slightly apart, she beheld what they were working on. Without meaning to, she gasped. For it was the most beautiful necklace she'd ever seen! Golden and hammered, it had fancy designs and was decorated with small, winking rubies and diamonds. But what caught her eye was the single large jewel that dangled at its center. It was shaped like a teardrop. It was walnut size and stunningly beautiful. It was *Brising*! She'd come to the right place!

At her gasp the dwarfs jumped around to gaze at her in surprise. Now one of them bellowed, "WHAT DO YOU WANT?" Based on the portraits, this was Berling.

Freya stepped forward. "Can I buy that necklace

you're making?" she asked, even though she hadn't brought any money.

"Negative," grumped Alfrigg. "Go away."

"But you stole—" Freya stopped herself just in time. She doubted they'd simply return Brising if she told them it was hers. Instead their price might go up, since they'd guess how badly she wanted her jewel back. And if she got too pushy, they might run away with it. Brising could be lost to her forever!

She circled closer, keeping her eye on the necklace. Should she try to grab it and run? Were dwarfs fast runners? She didn't know. But everyone knew they loved gold.

"I'll trade you my gold chain," Freya offered.

"A GOLD CANE?" shouted Berling, looking around. "WHERE IS IT? I DON'T SEE IT!" Apparently, he had trouble hearing.

"No, a chain!" She tugged her broken chain from the tortoiseshell clasps that fastened it in place. "It's my best one. You're welcome to have it if you'll give me the necklace, or at least that big jewel there in its middle." This delicate chain was the last reminder she had of Brising. If she lost both it *and* her jewel to these dwarfs, it would be terribly sad. But it was a chance she had to take.

"The jewel is worth far more than that chain. Besides, it's not for sale. Why do you want it so much, anyway?" Dvalin asked suspiciously.

"Because it's pretty?" she said, trying to sound casual. But she had already acted too anxious.

Alfrigg frowned. "We have lots of other pretty jewels lying around the forge," he snapped. "We'll trade you for one of those!"

Grerr narrowed his eyes. "There must be something special about this teardrop jewel, since she wants it so badly." He sounded as suspicious as Dvalin had.

Berling had been cupping his ears in an effort to hear better. "MAYBE IT'S MAGIC!" he yelled.

All four dwarfs began coaxing the jewel to do magic.

"Come on, jewely-wuly."

"Show us some magicky-wagicky."

Dvalin pulled off his leather glove to cup the jewel in his bare palm. To Freya's surprise, Brising did not change color in reaction to his mood. It remained as clear as a diamond. Oh no! Was it broken?

"We'll polish you to a high shine as a reward," Grerr promised the jewel.

When still nothing happened, Berling yelled at it. "DO SOMETHING, YOU DUMB OL' JEWEL!" Insults did no good either.

"That sparkly rock's a dud," grouched Alfrigg.

Has my jewel's magic been broken by its fall from the bridge? Freya worried. No matter, she still wanted to rescue it. It wasn't just a piece of rock to her. It was a friend! And like Ratatosk's squirrely message acorn had said the other day, friends were more important than anything.

 198

"HEY! DID YOU MAKE THAT EAR WARMER?" Berling asked out of nowhere. He was pointing at the lopsided, pointy-ended pouch Ms. Frigg had knitted.

"You mean this?" Freya asked, lifting the red knit pouch from its bead necklace in surprise. He nodded with such excitement that she handed it to him for a closer look. Berling promptly set the pointy pouch over his ear, saying, "IT'S A PERFECT FIT!"

"Let me see it," said Dvalin, snatching the "ear warmer" Berling now wore. One by one the dwarfs began trying it on, each looking thrilled with it.

"Could you knit us ear warmers like this?" Grerr asked in excitement. "All in different colors?"

"Ooh! Yeah! Like the ones our mommy knitted for us when we were little dwarfies, remember?" enthused a suddenly ungrouchy Alfrigg.

"Too bad they wore out," said Dvalin.

"And we don't know how to knit more," added Grerr. Reluctantly he tossed the pouch back to her,

and she replaced it on its beaded chain.

"Sure, I could get you more ear warmers like this, no problem," Freya offered quickly. "Let's make a deal. Two ears times four dwarfs equals eight. So eight knitted warmers in trade for the necklace?" She crossed her fingers. This seemed her only hope of rescuing Brising!

Although she didn't have a clue how to knit something quite as, er, quirky as these pointy ear-warmer pouches herself, she knew someone who did. Ms. Frigg! She had said she especially enjoyed knitting replacements for things that others had lost. And the ear warmers knitted by the dwarfs' mommy were things they'd lost to childhood, right? Freya felt sure that once she explained, Ms. Frigg would be touched and agree to knit replacements.

The dwarfs huddled up to discuss the matter, then broke apart again. "Deal!" Alfrigg declared. From the sly way he and the others were looking at one another, they appeared to think the bargain was in their favor. And maybe it was. What use was one more necklace to them, no matter how pretty? It wouldn't keep their ears warm!

Delighted, Freya reached for the necklace. However, Alfrigg snatched it away. For a moment she had touched her jewel, though, and it had flashed with color. So its magic wasn't entirely broken after all. Still, it must be damaged somehow, since it hadn't worked for the dwarfs earlier. She hoped she'd be able to repair it.

"EAR WARMERS FIRST," Berling insisted.

"Then you'll get the necklace," Dvalin informed her.

Nooo! She couldn't leave without Brising! Darkalfheim dwarfs were known to break deals if a better one came along. *She* wouldn't back out on this deal, but what if *they* did before she could return?

"Can't I take the necklace now? I'll bring the ear warmers soon. Promise," she told them.

The dwarfs crossed their arms and shook their heads. "Nope," Alfrigg said, grumpy again. "That's not how we do business."

No sooner had he said this than, seemingly out of nowhere, a golden-bristled boar broke into the forge. It began racing around, knocking over tools and crashing into things.

"Drat! Those rotten blacksmiths Brokk and Sindri are practicing boar making again. This one's crazier than the last *boar*ing prototype they made!" Alfrigg shouted.

"Get out!"

"Back off, boar!"

Waving their arms, the four dwarfs chased the boar, trying to shoo it out of their workshop without getting stuck by its sharp tusks.

Suddenly the boar wheeled about to chase *them*. "Yikes!" yelled Grerr. The dwarfs made an abrupt U-turn and took off running the other way, deeper into the caves. Alfrigg wasn't fast enough, though. *Oomph!* The boar head-butted him in the rear.

"Yeow!" *Clink!* Alfrigg dropped the necklace to the floor but kept running.

As the boar herded the dwarfs away, Freya grabbed the necklace and fled the cave. "Don't worry! I'll bring the ear warmers. You can trust me. I'm just not sure I can trust you!" she called over her shoulder.

The dwarfs were so busy escaping the boar that they didn't even reply!

14
Trickery

FREYA FOUND HER WAY OUT OF THE Darkalfheim tunnels with no trouble. Outside the cave's entrance the rocky path before her sloped downhill. She paused to catch her breath, glad to note that the dwarfs had not yet come after her.

She gazed lovingly at the jewel in the center of the beautiful necklace she held. *Success!* In a single day she'd gotten Brising back, plus made contact with Gullveig. All that was left to do to complete her secret plan was talk Frey into going home to Vanaheim!

As she held her jewel, it flashed shades of blue and purple. It was happy! "Me too. I promise I'll never lose you again," she whispered to Brising, gently rubbing the jewel with her fingertip. To her delight, it warmed, but instead of showing her a vision, it spoke a future-telling:

"Promise made by words you've spoken
Within minutes will be broken."

Hmm. "I think your future-telling skills are still a little off, Brising. I'll keep my promise to the dwarfs. They'll get those ear warmers even if I have to knit them myself!" But wait. Had her jewel meant her other promise? The one she'd made to never lose it again? "Don't worry," she assured it just in case. "See? I'm putting you on now. You're safe with me."

As Freya lifted the dwarf-made necklace to clasp it around her throat, she felt a sharp pinch on her neck. A flea had bitten her. "Ow!" Her hands flew out, reaching toward the bite . . . and she dropped Brising! *Nooo!* Not *again*!

The necklace tumbled down the slope, coming to rest on a large rock. Quickly she ran and bent to retrieve it. However, the flea was faster. It hopped from her to the necklace, where it transformed into . . . Loki?

Grinning at her like this was all some big joke, he grabbed the necklace and sailed off, now in the form of a big gray bird.

Huh? That annoying boygod could shape-shift? Somehow he'd found her here, decided to turn himself into a flea to bug her into dropping the Brising necklace, and then transformed again so he could steal it. Well, he wasn't going to get away with this.

"You! Flea-bird boy!" she shouted after him, shaking her fist in the air. "Give me back my necklace! This is not funny! I mean it!"

But Loki just kept flying, with the necklace in his

beak. Well, little did he know that she had the means to fly as well. Quickly Freya pulled her cat's-eye marble from its pouch and tossed it high.

Plink! The marble landed on the snowy ground and instantly transformed into her tabby cats and cart. *Meow! Meow!*

In minutes she was zooming through the air in the cart, her long, glittering hair fanning out behind her. Since she wasn't all that confident in her flying skills yet, she stayed low, traveling only a few dozen feet above the snowy ground.

When she reached the first ring and passed over Heimdall at his post on the Bifrost Bridge, she waved to him. He looked surprised to see her flying. However, recognizing her, he beckoned her onward. Loki was so far ahead by now that she'd almost lost sight of him. Judging from his flight path, she guessed he was planning to land at Valaskjalf, where she'd first met Odin and Ms. Frigg. Weird choice! Still, she would follow him there, even if it would take her higher than she'd ever flown. She had to rescue Brising . . . again!

Uh-oh! As she neared the platform in Yggdrasil's topmost branches, she saw she'd miscalculated. She was coming in too fast. It was going to take all her limited skill not to crash-land!

"Whoa, kitty, kitty!" she shouted desperately. Her cats banked against the wind to help slow them. Would it be enough? *Thump!* They landed. Claws out, the cats skidded to a halt at the base of the steps up to the two thrones. Ms. Frigg (who was knitting twinkly stars and releasing them into the heavens) and Odin looked at her in surprise. Loki, too, for he had already transformed to his boygod self and was speaking to Odin—who was holding Brising!

Meow! Meow!

"Good job, *silfrkatter*," Freya said, leaping from her cart. She gave her cats pets and kisses. Then she said the magic word: "Catnap!" *Plink!* She snatched the cat's-eye marble from the air, then plunked it back into its pouch.

Odin had been examining her necklace, but now he leaned to discuss it with Ms. Frigg. Her needles kept clicking as she replied in low-voiced words Freya couldn't hear.

What was going on here? Had Loki claimed the necklace was his, and come to show it off or give it to them as a gift?

"That necklace is mine!" Freya announced in a strong, determined voice. "Loki took it from me."

Odin startled her by saying, "Yes, I know. I asked him to bring it here."

"But why?" she asked, totally puzzled now. Loki snickered.

Odin straightened with a frown and nodded sternly to the boygod. Seeming to understand that this was an instruction to depart, Loki shape-shifted into a bird again, sent her a cocky, beaky grin, and then flew away.

Good riddance, in her opinion! She eyed her necklace, which Odin was now idly tossing a few inches in the air, then catching in his palm over and over again.

"The way you acted when I asked about your magic yesterday seemed suspicious," Odin announced once Loki was gone. "And with the history of mistrust between Asgard and Vanaheim, I thought I'd better find out if you were up to something. So when I discovered you were on your way to Darkalfheim, I asked Loki to follow you and see what he could learn."

"But . . ." Freya shifted from one foot to the other, wanting to ask how he'd discovered where she'd gone. It didn't really matter, she supposed. He could've used his amazing telescope. Or his awesome single-eye sight. Or even his ravens. Odin had his ways, and he probably wouldn't reveal them to her even if she dared to ask.

"Well? EXPLAIN YOURSELF!" Odin shouted.

His loud command jolted her into instantly blurting out the truth. "When I was up here before, you said you and Ms. Frigg brought me to the academy because of my magic. I was scared to tell you that I don't have any of my own. Brising—the jewel in the center of that necklace—is the one with the magic." *Uh-oh!* What had she just done? She clapped her hand over her mouth, wishing she could call back the words.

"I'd guessed as much," Odin said, surprising her. "That's why I had Loki bring the jewel to me. Before you arrived just now, I tried with all my might to make its magic work. As did Loki and Frigg." He paused for a suspenseful moment and then added, "Nothing happened."

"Huh?" Freya glanced at Ms. Frigg.

"You and that jewel? It seems you're partners. A team, neither able to do future-telling magic without the other," Ms. Frigg explained.

When Odin handed the necklace containing Brising back to Freya, she gazed upon her jewel with new wonder. "So that's why the dwarfs couldn't make your magic work . . . partner," she murmured, touched and pleased with this news. Feeling even closer to her dear jewel now, she clasped its necklace around her throat, where it flashed colors of deep contentment.

Odin smiled. "Every student we invited to Asgard Academy has some unique kind of special magic to offer. Like your brother Frey's ability to help things grow, for example. Or the magic to bring snow." That magic belonged to the frost giants, Freya knew, recalling how they'd shaken snow from their white hair.

"And with others, like you, it's a specialness you have within yourself," said Ms. Frigg.

"Um . . ." Freya cocked her head at them. She didn't exactly understand what they were getting at.

Odin regarded her keenly. "Did you think Ms. Frigg and I brought you all the way to Asgard just because of your ability to foretell the future?"

"You didn't?" Freya stared at him in surprise.

After exchanging a look with Ms. Frigg, Odin smiled again and leaned forward in his throne. "Never underestimate your abilities, Freya. Though it does take great skill to coax magic from a jewel, we had a bigger reason for inviting you. Your *special* ability to foster friendship."

"And that natural skill is its own kind of magic," added Ms. Frigg.

Till now Freya *had* assumed it was only her power to see the future that had caused Odin and Ms. Frigg to bring her here. Their words made her happy heart sing with even greater joy!

Odin sat back in his throne. "Now Ms. Frigg and I have work to do. So off with you! And stay out of trouble. I'll be watching," he warned. The sky-blue door appeared then, a hint that she should depart.

"Um, can I ask a favor first?" Freya asked Ms. Frigg. When the coprincipal looked up from her knitting, Freya quickly explained about the dwarfs' having "lost" the ear warmers their mom had made for them. As she'd

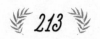

hoped, the kindhearted Ms. Frigg immediately offered to knit new ones and have Odin's ravens deliver them to Darkalfheim. She began work on them before Freya was even out the blue door!

Moments later Freya was stepping from the portal onto the fernway that led to the Valhallateria. Immediately some all-too-familiar sounds greeted her. *Crunch! Bam! Snort!*

Argh! With everything that had happened, she'd managed again to put Mason's building project out of her mind for a time. But from here she could see that his wall was *waaay* taller now. And he was still working. In fact, the sounds of his sledgehammer striking stone continued through that night and all of Saturday, too. It was giving her a headache!

By Sunday the wall was nearing completion. After breakfast Freya took the trail over to Yggdrasil's trunk to the place where the little slot door had appeared before.

"Gullveig! Hey! I'm in trouble and need some advice! Also, I need to tell you that the war's over and Odin thinks you stole Asgard's gold," she called out desperately.

Nothing. No matter how much she knocked, Gullveig didn't seem to hear. Probably busy with that noisy water slide or her wands or something. But Freya wasn't giving up. At the very least she needed to fix things between Gullveig and Odin. Quickly, she gathered some twigs and used them to construct this message in the snow, hoping her *amma* would find it: *War over. Can I tell O where U R?*

That done, she hurried off to look for Frey. Since Gullveig and Mimir weren't around, she would seek her brother's opinion on what to do. Unfortunately, he and his new buddies from Tree Lore class had gone off on a weekend campout to give aid to a field of blighted cloudberries near the border between Midgard and Jotunheim. While that was admirable and made her proud of him, it also frustrated her. With a sigh she headed back to Vingolf.

As a heavy snow began to fall, she and most of the AA girls hunkered down in the dorm. Freya flopped onto her podbed and eyed her roommates. Skade was inspecting the binding on her skis, Sif was straightening her stash of hair ribbons, and Idun was reading a runebook about fruit. They were all super nice. She remembered how they had oohed and aahed over her new necklace when they saw it, making her feel special. And she really needed to talk her worries over with somebody, so . . .

"I bet this weather'll slow down Mason's wall," Sif remarked, giving her an opening.

Instantly Freya's mood improved. "You think?" She was about to ask for their advice on what to do if he somehow did succeed, when Skade suggested, "Want to play a game? It might help take your mind off all that."

"Ooh! I love games!" said Freya. Skade was right.

 216

She needed something to take her mind off the wall. And games were fun! She hopped up. "Let's go ask some of the other girls to play too, okay?"

Minutes later, she had organized a game of charades out in the main area, suggesting topics such as famous heroes, geographic locations, gods, goddesses, and Ymir. Most of the pods participated, and some world groups actually started cross-bonding and laughing together. It was really too bad that when the girlgiants began losing, they started an argument that brought the game to an abrupt end. Still, it had been a start at cross-world friend making!

Finally the snow let up. While everyone else went to the V for lunch, Freya grabbed one of Idun's apples and headed off to see if Gullveig was back. The snow was thick on the ground now. So thick that it had completely covered up the twigs she'd used to leave her message! She walked along the trunk of Yggdrasil one way and then the other. But things looked different with the new snow somehow, and she couldn't find the entrance to the library. Did that also mean she'd lost Gullveig again? Forever?

She noticed something glinting under the snow next to the tree. When she kneeled for a closer look and brushed the snow aside, she found pieces of Asgard gold! They'd been laid to form a rune that meant "yes"! This had to be Gullveig's reply to the message Freya had left, letting her know it was okay to tell Odin about her and Mimir and their library in the tree. Which also meant this part of the tree must be where the slot sometimes appeared.

That was great, but she still would've liked to see Gullveig to ask her advice about Mason. Standing, she raised her hand to knock.

Caw! Just then Odin's ravens flew overhead. Each held one end of a long strand of yarn stretched between their beaks, from which hung four pairs of pointy, lopsided ear warmers of various colors. They must be taking them to the dwarfs. Wow! Ms. Frigg was fast at knitting!

Freya waved the two ravens closer. "I have a message for Odin!" Hearing her, one of the ravens passed off its end of the yarn to the other raven, which continued on toward Darkalfheim with the ear warmers. After the empty-beaked raven swooped down and landed on a nearby branch, Freya told it about Mimir and Gullveig and their library, and how they'd thought they were helping Odin by hiding Asgard's gold and hadn't known the war had ended. Then she tossed one piece of gold to the raven as evidence that her story was true.

"*Caw*t it!" said the raven, having done just that, the piece of gold now clamped neatly in one claw. As it winged back in the direction of Valaskjalf, Freya heard Mason pounding on the wall again. She shuddered.

Gazing down at her jewel, which now hung from the new necklace she wore, she asked, "What's going to happen, Brising? Will Mason finish the wall by tonight?" Since she no longer had to pull her jewel out of a pouch, it was way easier to speak to. The fact that its changing colors revealed her mood was something that, luckily, no one had yet figured out.

Brising replied:

> *"What will happen is not known.*
> *It will depend on gold and stone."*

"On Asgard's gold, you mean? And on the stones Mason is using to build the wall?" she asked it. But Brising revealed no more.

Oh, how she wished her jewel had been able to reassure her that Mason would fail! She sighed. For a moment she considered escaping the situation by running back to Vanaheim. But that would be cowardly. Besides, she couldn't leave before Frey returned from his plant-helping mission. If only she could come up with an honorable way to get out of that promise she'd made to Mason. It made her cringe to think of promising her heart to him in front of everyone, especially her new friends and a certain cute hay-haired boy she'd met on the bridge!

She studied her surroundings carefully before leaving this time, making sure she wouldn't lose the library entrance ever again. Then she took the remaining gold pieces still glinting in the snow and arranged them in the rune for her name. That way Gullveig would know she'd gotten the message. There was one piece left over.

As she examined the palm-size gold piece, an idea as bright as gold came to her. Smiling to herself, she pocketed the piece and headed for the dorm. Because now she had a new secret plan!

15
The Wall

SUNDAY AFTERNOON FLEW BY. DINNERTIME—
Mason's deadline for finishing the wall—was fast
approaching. Freya put away the tool she'd been using
from her Findings class and stood back to gaze upon
the palm-size gold piece that now lay on her podbed in
Vingolf Hall.

With time running out, all the other students had
already gone down to the wall to see if the boygiant
would finish in time. Now she would go too. First,

however, she opened her closet and slipped a berry-red dress on over her woolen shift and stockings. Then she applied matching berry-red lip gloss. As the girlgoddess of love and *beauty*, she wanted to look her best, even if this turned out to be a disaster!

Lastly, she tucked the gold piece into one of her pouches and left the girls' dorm. On her way to the Bifrost Bridge, she was surprised to come upon a new sign along the fernway that read:

THE HEARTWOOD LIBRARY
Knowledge Is Power

Below that was an arrow pointing in the direction of Yggdrasil's trunk. This must mean that Gullveig and Mimir had already made up with Odin! That they'd reminded him of his long-ago request that Mimir take care of Asgard's gold in the event of war, and had explained how Gullveig had only been helping him.

Odin had obviously realized it was all a misunderstanding. Because it appeared the library was now open to students!

Stepping a little lighter at this news, Freya continued over the bridge, down to where her fate would unfold. It looked like the whole student body had gathered by the wall to see what would happen. Villagers from other worlds had heard about the bet and come too. Skade, Idun, and Sif must've been watching for Freya, because they rushed to greet her.

"You okay?" asked Idun.

Freya nodded. Giving her podmates a brave smile, she turned to watch the work in progress. Instantly her smile turned upside down. As it must've been before the war, the wall now stood tall and strong. And in spite of today's snowy-weather setback, it looked complete!

She gasped. "Mason finished?"

"Not quite yet. See?" said Sif. She pointed to one last chink in the wall that needed to be filled.

Freya's stomach tightened as she watched Mason's brown-and-white horse lift a huge stone and head for the wall to fill in the chink. Who needed Ragnarok? It looked like her own personal doomsday was right around the corner!

Snort! Before Unlucky could reach the wall, a new black horse suddenly galloped out of the nearby forest. Upon seeing the new horse, Unlucky let out a happy whinny, as if to say, *Oh boy, a playmate!* Dropping the stone, he galloped off with the black horse to frolic in the forest.

"Come back!" Mason called after his horse. But apparently, Unlucky was done with wall building for now. Mason enlarged to giant size and tried to pick up the huge stone himself, but it was too heavy, even for a giant. He released it and shrank himself back down.

Tooot! Heimdall sounded his horn to signal that the deadline had passed.

"Time's up!" whooped Skade.

Relief flooded Freya. There was still one hole left in the wall. Mason had failed!

Suddenly the two horses came galloping back. *What dark-blue eyes that black one has,* Freya thought as it passed her. Both horses stopped right in front of Mason. Without warning, the black one shape-shifted into Loki!

Losing interest now that the black horse was gone, Unlucky went over to the wall and pushed the final stone into place. The wall was finished! But it was too late for Mason to win the bet. The poor guy looked so disappointed that Freya instantly felt sorry for him.

A cheer went up from the Asgard students and villagers when they realized the wall was complete.

Sif's mouth fell open. "Loki saved the day!" she said in disbelief.

"Yeah, just when you think that boygod is a total dweeb, he goes and does something nice," said Skade from beside her.

"Ha-ha! Tricked you!" the girls heard Loki tease Mason.

"And then he does something kind of mean again," Freya added, rolling her eyes.

"Cheater!" Mason yelled at Loki, who was laughing now. To his credit, the boygiant didn't take his anger at Loki out on his horse. Instead he gave him a pat and whispered something in his ear. *Schmop!* Unlucky shrank back into a horse carving, which Mason strung on the cord about his neck again.

"So Loki came to the rescue, huh? You never know what to expect from that guy," a familiar voice said from beside Freya.

She swung around to see Frey, looking tired but happy. There were twigs stuck in his hair. "You're back from camping!" she said.

"Yeah. Did I miss anything? Besides Loki's horse trick?" He gestured toward a group of frost giants. "Those guys sure don't look happy about it."

Sure enough, the giant students among them were grumbling and eyeing both the Vanir and Aesir with hostility.

"They never like it when anyone from Jotunheim gets tricked by the gods," Skade said. She shrugged. "Being part giant, I understand."

"I can understand them being mad too," said Idun. "Poor Mason."

"Yeah, he worked so hard, only to have Loki bamboozle him in the end," added Sif. Glancing at Freya, she added quickly, "But for your sake I'm glad Loki did what he did, of course."

"Me too," said Frey. "But I can see why he and the other giants don't think things turned out fair."

That was all Freya needed to hear. What her brother and roomies had said confirmed her own feelings. Even though Mason hadn't succeeded, she decided to put the plan she'd come up with earlier that day into action. She just hoped it would smooth things over with him—with everybody, really!

She felt everyone's eyes on her as she went over to the wall and stepped up beside the shaggy-haired boy-giant. Speaking loudly so that all would hear, she made a formal announcement. "Mason, we are all grateful to you for rebuilding the wall. In return for your effort, I will give you the sun and the moon, as promised. And . . ." She paused dramatically, then went on, "I will give you my heart!"

A gasp rose from the crowd. Surprised, Mason grinned at her happily. Then he closed his eyes and leaned forward, puckering up.

She leaned back. *Whoa!* He hoped for a kiss? Well, *she* hoped he and the other giant students from Jotunheim wouldn't be too disappointed—or angry—when she gave him something else instead.

"The heart I give you is not the fickle kind whose fleeting affection doesn't last," she continued, still speaking loudly enough for all to hear. "What I'm offering you is one you can keep with you for always."

Mason opened his eyes and straightened, looking puzzled now.

Taking a fortifying breath, Freya pulled the palm-size gold piece from her pouch. She handed it to Mason and, with great flair, bent low in a curtsy.

"Gold?" he said, sounding a little insulted. "You're paying me?"

"Note its shape," she told him, straightening. She drew an invisible heart shape in the air between them with one fingertip.

He nodded, unimpressed. "Oh, I get it. The gold is shaped like a heart."

"Which symbolizes *my* heart. By building this wall, you have earned my heartfelt thanks, freely given. And see?" she said eagerly. "Not only did I shape it into a heart, but I engraved runes on each side. A moon and a sun. Please accept this gift as your reward for a job well done."

When he still looked unsure and a little downcast, she rushed on. "You've won more than just my heart today, you know. You've won the hearts of everyone here at Asgard Academy. From the bottoms of our hearts, we all thank you," she finished kindly.

Mason turned the heart-shaped gold piece over and over in his fingers, studying it for long seconds. *Why doesn't he speak?* Freya began to wonder anxiously. Was he going to reject her offering?

Suddenly a big smile crossed his face, and he wrapped his fingers tight around the heart, waving it high in victory. "Freya gave me her heart, with a rune of the sun and the moon!" he shouted to one and all. "Hey, I rhymed. I'm a poet like Odin and didn't know it!" He ran off toward the academy with his gold heart gift, kicking up his heels and looking delighted.

Phew! thought Freya, *heart*ily glad. Gullveig had come to this world seeking gold to make Freya happy. And in the end a single piece of that gold had brought

231

more happiness to all the worlds than either of them could ever have imagined. The kind of happiness that came from the hope of peace, at least for now.

Since the show was over, villagers began to amble away, chatting with one another a mile a minute about what had happened there. Soon only students remained. Many of them gathered around Freya and congratulated her on having come up with such a brilliant, satisfying idea. Her three podmates sent her thumbs-ups from the wall, where they and others stood admiring it. When Loki and Od drifted near, Freya thanked Loki for his trick.

"No prob," he said casually, before heading off to inspect the wall up close and tease some light-elf girls. Which left her and Od standing together.

Before either could speak, Odin and Ms. Frigg appeared atop the newly rebuilt wall. Seeing them up there, Freya remembered that poem Odin had seemed to want her to supply a rhyming word for when they first met:

Breaking branch, or flaring flame,

Freya of all-seeing fame,

Welcome to my throne and hall.

Have you come to fix our . . . ?

She had failed to guess an answer then, but now one came to her: wall! He'd wanted the wall fixed, and now it was. And it was *sort of* due to her presence here that Mason had wound up fixing it!

Odin's voice boomed suddenly, snapping her out of her thoughts. "Welcome, students of Asgard Academy! By now you have completed your first days at the academy. As you know, we invited you all here from many different worlds for a purpose," he said while stroking the ravens on each of his shoulders. "It is our sincere hope that you will strive to work well together, so you may serve as a good example to others. For you have the power to inspire all nine worlds to live forever in peace and harmony!"

"Which is good for Yggdrasil!" Frey shouted out.

"Yes!" Odin cheered. He punched both fists so high and hard that the ravens on his shoulders flapped away and went to circle overhead.

"Now, I know it's a big adjustment for you being among so many new faces here at Asgard Academy," Odin went on. "So I have some advice." Pausing, he got that faraway look Freya remembered from her first visit to his hall. She thought she knew what that look meant, and sure enough, he launched into a new poem:

> *"You didn't ask to come to this place,*
> *Where everything may seem strange.*
> *But with the help of newfound friends*
> *It could be a wonderful . . ."*

"Change!" Freya yelled in unison with almost every single student at the wall. The fact that they'd all been able to supply the correct word to him right away made her realize something. That other students probably felt the same way *she* did about leaving their homes and their former friends and lives behind. Like Odin had said, being among new faces wasn't easy. Given enough time, would all these students grow used to the change and begin to mingle and mix? She hoped so. Then maybe, just maybe, the academy would start to feel more like home to them all. But was she prepared to call it home herself?

As Freya considered this, Ms. Frigg spoke up. "Students, we now ask that each of you please turn to someone standing close by, someone you don't yet know well, and introduce yourself."

At this request the majority of the students shared quick, shy, excited, nervous glances at those standing near them.

Woo-hoo! Od was still standing next to Freya, and since she really only barely knew him, Freya stuck out her hand so they could shake. "Very nice to meet you,

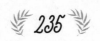

235

Freya," Od told her, even though he already knew her name, of course. He pumped her hand up and down.

"Right back at you," she replied, which made him laugh. He thought her funny? This made her feel like doing one of the light-elves' happy dances. Then and there she vowed she would not wash that hand for a whole year if she could help it!

After these introductions were made, Ms. Frigg went on. "Now, students, please turn in a new direction. Shake hands and introduce yourself to someone else you don't know well."

When Freya turned, her smile drooped at the sight of Angerboda, who had the exact same drooping-smile reaction upon seeing *her*. Recovering quickly, however, Freya reached out her hand. And to her surprise, so did Angerboda. But before their palms could connect, Angerboda whipped hers up to smooth her own snow-white hair back. It had been a sneaky fake-out handshake, clearly meant to embarrass Freya.

Some friendships wouldn't come easily, it seemed. Freya hoped Odin and Ms. Frigg knew that. She smiled big at Angerboda anyway. It was clearly not the reaction the girlgiant had expected, and she almost smiled back! But she caught herself in the nick of time and walked off with her nose in the air.

Freya's smile just got bigger. Because she had *almost* gotten Angerboda to smile! It was at that very moment that Freya made a decision to embrace her changed life. Once and for all, she abandoned her secret plan to return to Vanaheim. She and her brother could do more good here. Like he was fond of saying, they would bloom where they were planted. Here at Asgard Academy!

16
Clomp!

Tooot! **A WEEK LATER FREYA, SIF, IDUN,** and Skade were returning from Midgard Mall via the Bifrost Bridge when they heard Heimdall's horn calling everyone to dinner. Freya had gotten separated from her podmates when she stopped to fish a pebble from her boot. Now she ran to rejoin them.

"Let's beat everyone else to the V!" she yelled as she caught up. The four girls took off like the wind. *Clomp! Clomp!* Freya was pleased to note that her podmates' boots made almost as much noise as hers!

"So you're what all the racket is!" boomed Heimdall as the foursome clattered to a stop at the top of the bridge. "I thought a storm was coming! You girls sound like thunder in those boots."

"We're hungry!" Freya exclaimed.

"You *did* call us to dinner," Skade added.

"So I did," chuckled Heimdall. Stepping aside, he gestured toward the golden doors. "Power on, thunder-girls!"

That's it! thought Freya as they tumbled through the portal.

"Hey! Remember how we wanted a strong pod name?" she said to the others the second they landed on the fernway that would take them to the Valhallateria.

They all nodded. "Well, what says girl power more than *thunder*?" she hinted, waiting for them to catch on.

Light dawned in the other three girls' eyes. "You mean . . . THUNDER GIRLS?" they shouted in unison. Jumping around happily, they yelled out things like "Yeah!" "Perfect!" "Love it!"

"Woo-hoo!" Freya shouted. "We are the mighty Thunder Girls!"

"Blunder Girls?" echoed a squirrelly voice from somewhere up in Yggdrasil's branches. "That's what you named your pod? Weird, but whatever. I must go tell everyone!"

"Look—Ratatosk!" said Idun, pointing.

"Ymir's ears! He heard us wrong. And now he's off to tell the worlds the wrong pod name for us," said Sif.

"No! We're the Thunder Girls!" Skade called after him. The girls started clomping and waving, causing Ratatosk to look back.

"Yeah, I heard you! *Lumber* Girls it is!" Ratatosk assured them, still rushing away atop a wide branch. The girls groaned at the squirrel's botched attempts to get their name right. But then they all started to laugh.

"Hey! Let's show that squirrelly Ratatosk some of

our power right now," Freya said to her friends. "Our pod name on three. All together, okay?"

"One! Two! Three!" they counted aloud. Then they all four punched fists into the air like Odin had done a week earlier on the wall. Their yell, when it came, shook the leaves on the branches around them and caused Ratatosk to almost topple off the branch he was traveling on. No way he'd missed that. For they'd yelled their new name loud and proud, and with all their might:

"THUNDER GIRLS!"

Authors' Note

To WRITE EACH BOOK IN THE THUNDER GIRLS series, we choose one or more Norse myths and then give them an updated middle-grade twist. After deciding on what elements we'll include from various retellings of the myths, we freely add interesting and funny details in order to create meaningful and entertaining stories we hope you'll enjoy.

We also write the Goddess Girls middle-grade

series, which features Greek mythology. So why write another kind of mythology now too? Good question! Our enthusiasm for Norse mythology strengthened after Suzanne began frequent visits to her daughter and granddaughter, who live in Oslo, Norway. There, representations of the Norse gods and goddesses and their myths are found in many museums. Along the walls in the courtyard of the Oslo City Hall, there are painted wooden friezes (by painter and sculptor Dagfin Werenskiold) that illustrate motifs from various Norse myths. These friezes are the inspiration for the Valhallateria friezes that come alive at the end of meals in Thunder Girls!

We hope our series will motivate you to seek out actual retellings of Norse myths, which will also give you more understanding of and "inside information" about characters, myths, and details we've woven into Thunder Girls. Below are some of the sources we consult to create our stories.

- *D'Aulaires' Book of Norse Myths* by Ingri and Edgar Parin D'Aulaire (for young readers)
- *The Norse Myths* by Kevin Crossley-Holland
- *The Prose Edda* by Snorri Sturluson
- *The Poetic Edda* translated and edited by Jackson Crawford
- *Norse Mythology: A Guide to the Gods, Heroes, Rituals, and Beliefs* by John Lindow
- *Norse Mythology A to Z* by Kathleen N. Daly

For more about the art and friezes at Oslo City Hall, visit theoslobook.no/2016/09/03/oslo-city-hall.

Happy reading!

Joan and Suzanne

Acknowledgments

Many thanks to our publisher, Aladdin/Simon & Schuster, and our editor, Alyson Heller, who gave an immediate and supportive yes to our idea to write a Norse mythology–based middle-grade series. Alyson edits both Goddess Girls and Heroes in Training, our ongoing Greek mythology–based series for children. We have worked with her for many years and feel very lucky to be doing another new series with her and the other fine folk at Aladdin.

They help make our words shine, design fabulous art to make our books stand out, and make every effort to see that our books reach as many readers as possible.

We are also indebted to our literary agent, Liza Voges. She has championed us in all our joint series ventures and worked hard on our behalf and on behalf of our books. Thank you, Liza!

We are grateful to Danish artist Pernille Ørum for her striking jacket for this first book in our Thunder Girls series, and we look forward to more of her jackets for other books in the series.

Finally, we thank our husbands, George Hallowell and Mark Williams, for offering advice when asked, troubleshooting computer problems, and just making our lives richer and easier. During hectic times in our writing schedules they're always good sports, taking up the slack of daily chores without complaint.

Glossary

NOTE: PARENTHESES INCLUDE INFORMATION specific to the Thunder Girls series.

Aesir: Norse goddesses and gods who live in Asgard

Alfheim: World on the first (top) ring where light-elves live

Alfrigg: One of the dwarf blacksmiths who help craft Freya's necklace

Amma: Means "grandmother" (nickname for Gullveig)

Angerboda: Loki's giantess wife whose name means "distress-bringer" (angry Asgard Academy student and girlgiant)

Asgard: World on the first (top) ring where Aesir goddesses and gods live

Berling: One of the dwarf blacksmiths who help craft Freya's necklace

Bifrost Bridge: Red, blue, and green rainbow bridge built by the Aesir from fire, air, and water

Bragi: God of poetry (student at Asgard Academy and boygod)

Breidablik Hall: Hall of the Norse god Balder (boys' dorm at Asgard Academy)

Brising: Freya's necklace, shortened from *Brísingamen* (Freya's magic jewel)

Brokk: Dwarf blacksmith who works with his brother, Sindri, in Darkalfheim

Darkalfheim: World on the second (middle) ring where dwarfs live

Dvalin: One of the dwarf blacksmiths who help craft Freya's necklace

Dwarfs: Short blacksmiths in Darkalfheim (some of whom attend Asgard Academy)

Frey: Vanir god of agriculture and fertility whose name is sometimes spelled Freyr, brother of Freya (Freya's twin brother and Asgard Academy student and boygod)

Freya: Vanir goddess of love and fertility (Vanir girlgoddess of love and beauty who is an Asgard Academy student)

Frigg: Goddess of marriage, who is Odin's wife (coprincipal of Asgard Academy with Odin)

Fire giants: Terrifying giants that live in Muspelheim

Frost giants: Descendants of Ymir from Jotunheim

Gladsheim Hall: Sanctuary where twelve Norse gods hold meetings (Asgard Academy's assembly hall)

Grerr: One of the dwarf blacksmiths who help craft Freya's necklace

Gullveig: Vanir sorceress whose gold-hunting in Asgard causes the Aesir-Vanir war (Freya and Frey's nanny and assistant librarian at the Heartwood Library)

Hangerock: Sleeveless apronlike dress, with shoulder straps that are fastened in front by clasps, that is worn over a long-sleeved linen shift

Heimdall: Watchman of the gods (security guard at Asgard Academy)

Helheim: World on the third (bottom) ring inhabited by the evil dead and ruled by a female monster named Hel

Hlidskjalf: Odin's throne

Hugin: One of Odin's two ravens whose name means "thought"

Idun: Aesir goddess who is the keeper of the golden apples of youth (Asgard Academy student and girl-goddess)

Ivaldi's Sons: Four dwarf blacksmiths that craft Freya's necklace—Alfrigg, Berling, Dvalin, and Grerr

Jotun: Norse word for "giant"

Jotunheim: World on the second (middle) ring where frost giants live

Kvasir: Vanir god sent to Asgard at the end of the Aesir-Vanir war who offered helpful information (Asgard Academy student and boygod from Vanaheim)

Light-elves: Happy Asgard Academy students from Alfheim

Loki: Troublemaking, shape-shifting god of fire (Asgard Academy student and boygod)

Midgard: World on the second (middle) ring where humans live

Mimir: Wise Aesir god who was beheaded and revived by Odin ("head" librarian at Asgard Academy)

Mimir's Well: Well of wisdom at the end of Yggdrasil's second root in Jotunheim

Munin: One of Odin's two ravens whose name means "memory"

Muspelheim: World on the third (bottom) ring where fire giants live

Nerthus: Freya and Frey's mother, a peace-bringing earth goddess who drives a cart pulled by cows

Nidhogg: Dragon that lives in Niflheim

Niflheim: World on the third (bottom) ring where the good dead are sent

Njord: Vanir god of the sea sent to Asgard after the Aesir-Vanir war (Asgard Academy student and boygod from Vanaheim)

Norse: Related to the ancient people of Scandinavia, a region in Northern Europe that includes Denmark, Norway, and Sweden and sometimes Finland, Iceland, and the Faroe Islands

Od: Norse god who is Freya's lost husband (Asgard Academy student and boygod who tends to get lost)

Odin: Powerful Norse god of war, wisdom, and poetry who watches over all nine worlds (coprincipal of Asgard Academy with his wife, Ms. Frigg)

Ragnarok: Prophesied doomsday when goddesses and gods will fight a fiery battle against evil that could destroy all nine Norse worlds

Ratatosk: Squirrel that runs up and down Yggdrasil spreading gossip and insults

Rudl: Norse folk dance

Runes: Ancient, magical Norse symbols carved in wood, stone, or metal and used like alphabet letters to form words

Sif: Golden-haired goddess of the harvest (Asgard Academy student and girlgoddess)

Sindri: Dwarf blacksmith who works with his brother, Brokk, in Darkalfheim

Skade: Goddess of skiing, sometimes spelled Skadi (Asgard Academy student and half-giant girl)

Thor: Superstrong Norse god of thunder and storms (Asgard Academy student and boygod)

Trolls: Subgroup of giants who live in Ironwood Forest near Midgard (barefoot troublemakers at Bifrost Bridge)

Valhalla: Huge room in Asgard where dead warriors feast and fight (Valhallateria, Asgard Academy's cafeteria)

Valkyries: Warrior maidens in winged helmets who choose which warriors will die in battle and then bring them to Valhalla (cafeteria ladies and workers in Asgard Academy's Valhallateria)

Vanaheim: World on the first (top) ring where Vanir goddesses and gods live

Vanir: Norse goddesses and gods that live in Vanaheim

Vingolf Hall: Goddesses' meeting hall at Asgard (girls' dorm at Asgard Academy)

Yggdrasil: Enormous ash tree that links all nine ancient Norse worlds, also called the World Tree (location of Asgard Academy)

Ymir: Very first frost giant whose body parts grew into the world of Midgard

About the Authors

JOAN HOLUB is the *New York Times* bestselling author of over 150 books for young readers, including *Little Red Writing*, *Zero the Hero*, *Mighty Dads*, *This Little Trailblazer: A Girl Power Primer*, and *What Is the Statue of Liberty?* She also coauthors the Goddess Girls series with the amazing Suzanne. Joan loves her home, friends, and cats, like Freya; enjoys apples, like Idun; can ski, though maybe not as well as Skade; and has amazing golden hair, like Sif. (Okay, so maybe she only *wishes* this last one were true!) Visit her at joanholub.com.

SUZANNE WILLIAMS is a former elementary school librarian and the author of over seventy books for children, including the award-winning picture books *Library Lil* (illustrated by Steven Kellogg) and *My Dog Never Says Please* (illustrated by Tedd Arnold) and several chapter book and middle-grade series. She coauthors the

Goddess Girls series with the fantastic Joan. Suzanne is excited to be cowriting a Norse mythology–based series, since she frequently travels from her home near Seattle to the Nordic country of Norway. She loves reading, being with family and friends, walking, and yoga. She isn't a skier, but she likes snow. And she wishes she could take classes at a school as magical as Asgard Academy. Visit her at suzanne-williams.com.